Unwind

Leigh Sharp

First Edition: 2025

ISBN (paperback): 979-8-9933702-0-0
ASIN: B0FVHZ83QT

Published by Leigh Sharp.

leighsharpauthor.com

For every girl who hasn't yet realized she deserves better

Note From the Author

Please protect your mental health. Though minimal, this book does delve into topics that may be triggering for some, including sexual assault, sexual manipulation, and suicidal ideation.

Playlist

1. i'm confident that i'm insecure - Lawrence

2. logical - Olivia Rodrigo

3. One Day - Tate McRae

4. For Life (Take You Out, Treat You Right) - Stephen Day

5. Lovesick - Jenna Raine

6. Kiss Me - Ed Sheeran

7. Infinitely Falling - Fly By Midnight

8. Hesitate - Jonas Brothers

1

I hate the snow. Probably as much as some people hate snakes, or cockroaches. Winters in Iowa are brutal, and it's probably the only thing I miss about North Carolina. Mostly, I hate drudging through it, even when it's a short walk across campus to my car. As I walk through the doors of the massive four-story library I've basically lived at for the last few months, I brace myself. The air *hurts* as it smacks me in the face. The campus is busier than I've seen it yet, with carloads of people returning from winter break. People smile or nod as I walk past them and even though I grew up not far from here, it still takes me by surprise how nice people are. Everyone at Duke was so intense. Most glared at you as you walked by, as if you were just one more person that could knock them down in class rankings. I make my way to the parking lot across the quad, hugging myself with crossed arms as I try to hold on to any bit of body heat I can. Between the recently modernized buildings and multitude of bare trees, it's windy as hell. I'd bet this place is beautiful during the summer, but the shade is very unwelcome right now.

The drive to the apartment is just as bleak as my walk to the car, though I can't tell if that's because of my mood lately, or because there are no signs of life during the winter. I suppose it could also be because of the loss of feeling in my toes, but I digress. I pass the same boring houses on boring streets, all so uniform in their neat lines, nearly touching each other like they're afraid of being alone. How do people live like that? I mean, apartment living isn't the best, but having a property that you own right on top of someone else that you don't know? Sounds like a nightmare to me.

When I walk through the door of the warm apartment, I inhale the scent of lilac and rainforest from the nearby candle warmer and take what feels like my first deep breath of the day. Skye has always known how to make a place feel like home, even when it is only a nine hundred square foot box. The absence of music signals that I am alone. She's probably with Aubrey, if I had to guess. I fucking hate being alone. I've kept myself so busy that I hardly ever have time to think, but when I'm left to my own devices, that's all I can seem to do. I belly flop onto my bed with a sigh. Between shifts at the library and the diner, my whole body aches, yet my brain won't stop replaying my time at Duke over and over.

I am ninety percent sure that I'm going crazy. At least that's how it feels, and I've certainly heard it from enough people over the last few months. I just couldn't stay there anymore. I missed my brother and Skye, and I *knew* I wouldn't be able to take many more of the looks I got after I ended things with James. If I'm being truly honest with myself, I knew from day one that I was in the wrong major, but I was determined not to change it and add even more time there. Of course, there was always the worry of what Mom might think... Nevertheless I transferred. Changed schools, changed my major, and moved closer to home. I couldn't have done it without Skye. She has always been supportive, but she knew from the beginning that James wasn't right for me. Hell, even *I* knew James wasn't right for me after a while, but he was stable and familiar. He was all I'd ever known. He's a nice enough guy, but I'm glad I realized I couldn't have gone through with it before I made a huge mistake. If I had stayed, I would be in a job that I hated and married to a man I just didn't love no matter how much I wanted to. Of course, there was a time when I *thought* I loved him. But that's the thing about trying to settle, you get really good at convincing yourself that everything is great.

I turn to lay on my back and look around my room. It's not the best place I've ever lived in, but how can I complain when Skye has been letting me live here rent-free while I get my bearings? I look over at the small, lonely poster from my favorite band and there's a part of me that misses my room back home. A good eye for decorating is something that Skye and Mom have in common. My walls at home were a light lavender color with a deep purple accent wall. Mom had hung fake ivy across the entire length of the dark wall and there was a large mirror on the opposite wall. It was cute, but my reading spot was by far my favorite part of my room. There was a large window with a built in seat and bookshelves framing the whole thing. My love for reading was born in that bay window. On weekends, I would read from sun up to sun down, soaking in any and all books I could find. My pitifully small bookshelf in the corner of the room definitely can't compare. When James and I moved in together, his parents furnished our apartment, so I found a cheap, used bookshelf online when I got here. It's filled with my favorites that I've already read a thousand times, while the books on my TBR list sit in a box collecting dust at my mom's house. It's not like I have the space for them or time to read anyways.

The first day of the semester is tomorrow so it's probably time to move past my shit and finally get fully unpacked and prepare for classes. Given everything that happened, I almost failed my first semester of my junior year before I dropped out. Now that I'm paying for school on my own, I can't afford for that to happen again. The two small boxes in the corner have been staring at me everyday for the past month since I moved in, filled with ghosts of the past. Why did I even bring them with me? I should have stored them at home where they couldn't haunt me daily. I take a steadying breath and head toward them when Skye yells out from her room next door, causing me to jump. I was so lost in my thoughts, I didn't even hear her come in.

"Are you dressed yet?"

I roll my eyes. We haven't spent much time together since I moved in a month ago. Between shifts at the library on campus and Joe's, a local diner, I've been putting in at least sixty hours a week easily. Skye's been trying to get me to go out on every rare night I've had off since I got here, but it's been especially annoying since her girlfriend, Aubrey, landed a lead in a musical at the local community theater. Normally I'm a sucker for musicals and would jump at the chance to see one, but with everything that's been going on I just don't feel like myself and I definitely don't want to be around anyone. Still, I know I can't keep putting off going out with her— especially now that last night was my final shift at Joe's until spring break.

"I told you, not tonight. Soon, I promise. I still have to finish unpacking and get ready for classes tomorrow."

"Mia," Skye whines, elongating my name. "Come on. What better way to celebrate the new school year than to go to a musical! We haven't been out *once* since you moved in. Plus, it's closing night. I *promised* Aubrey I'd be there and I don't want to go by myself again. She told me she *really* wants you to see it."

I walk to her room and lay on her bed, taking her pink, fluffy decorative pillow in my arms. Her room is the same ugly taupe color, but it's a little bigger than mine. She has pictures of her friends and family all over her walls along with fake plants and fairy lights. I throw my arm over my eyes dramatically and peek out from under my arm to look at her. She looks beautiful, as usual. She's already dressed to kill and she's brushing her long, platinum hair at her silver vanity. I watch as she brushes dark eye shadow on her eyelids and follows it with a line of black eyeliner, the colors making her hazel eyes pop. I swear, anyone else would look like a raccoon, but Skye pulls it off effortlessly. She catches my eye in the mirror, one eyebrow arched and a knowing smile playing on her lips—the kind that says she knows she's won.

"Fine," I whine. "But we're coming right back here after the show, deal?"

She squeals in excitement and rushes over to pull me to my feet before giving me a quick kiss on the cheek and an overly excited swat on the ass.

"Go get dressed!" she exclaims.

I chuckle and head to my own room to get ready. Looking through my small closet at the dresses and sweaters hanging, I'm overwhelmed. I never know what to wear to community theater. Do I dress up, wear something more casual, or meet somewhere in the middle?

Skye yells out at me to hurry as she wants to do my makeup, something she's always loved doing. I swear, she acts like I'm her own personal doll. I can already tell tonight is going to be a long one. I stand in front of my closet a few more minutes before I finally slide on an oversized blue knit sweater and baggy jeans.

"Mmm..." Skye appears in my doorway, taking in my outfit with squinted eyes. "Lose the jeans, but the sweater is cute. Here, put these on."

She tosses me a pair of skinny jeans that she'd walked in with that still has the tags on and I give her a disapproving glare.

Skye has been lucky in that she's never had to worry about money. Her parents aren't crazy rich or anything, but they've always been comfortable. At least, definitely more comfortable than my mom, brother, and I were. As a result, Skye is always trying to buy me things, passing them off as things she bought for herself that didn't fit– despite the fact that there is a four-size difference between us.

"What? I just haven't gotten around to wearing them yet! Put them on."

I hold them up to my hips in front of me, studying them. They're the right size on the tag, but they seem so much smaller.

"Listen, I love you, but we don't have time for you to second-guess it. Please just put them on." Skye gives my arm a reassuring squeeze before heading back to her room.

I step out of the jeans I was wearing and literally jump into the new ones. They're *tight* in all the wrong places, putting my thighs on display in a way that makes me pull at the fabric. I tug my sweater down, hoping that by some miracle I can make it stretch down to my knees. The fashion industry is the worst. Why is it that I can wear this same size in a different brand and they'll fit perfectly, but then there are jeans like these... Skye walks in with an approving look, makeup in hand, and dramatically gestures for me to sit at my desk. I do as I'm told and look up at her.

"You're going to love the show tonight," she gushes as she prepares her brush with a mocha color. "And I'm not just saying that because Aubrey is in it."

"I don't know," I breathe, closing my eyes. "I just have so much to do and I'm so nervous about tomorrow."

"Oh shush, it's going to be fine and you know it. I promise."

Skye gently blows on my face, trying to get the liquid liner she applied to dry faster. She pulls on my shoulders to get me to stand and walks me over to the mirror with my eyes still closed. I've pretty much got this ritual down pat at this point, knowing I'll get scolded if I open them before she's ready.

"Okay, open up, gorgeous lady," Skye gushes.

I look over myself in the mirror, running my fingers through my wildly wavy chestnut hair, so it's somewhat presentable. I run my eyes over my outfit again, and even though the jeans make my thighs look like they're going to burst through the seams at any moment, I feel like I actually look okay.

The entire ride to the theater is filled the latest pop hits at full blast. Skye doesn't know how to drive without the radio at top volume, and I can't help but get hyped when it is. I can't wait until it's warmer and we can drive with the windows down and the music blaring. We sing loudly, and slightly off key, right up until we're in the parking lot.

Skye and I take our seats near the middle. Others are still taking their seats as I flip through the program of *The Last Five Years,* which happens to be my favorite musical. Of course it's a two-hander, so there's just Aubrey and a guy named... Sunshine. I stifle a giggle. Who would do that to their kid? Poor guy.

"See? I told you you'd be excited," Skye whispers when she sees me smiling. "Aubrey is *amazing.*"

When the lights dim in the audience, my stomach flips in excitement. Something about being in a dark theater, knowing you're about to watch people give their best performances always gets me. When the lights come up on Aubrey, I can see a few tears rolling down her stoic face even from five rows back. Her voice is beautiful and she's a phenomenal actor.

Sunshine's tall, slim figure enters the stage for the next number and the moment he starts singing, I swear my jaw nearly drops to the floor. With looks like that, he could literally be named Shitbag and I bet he'd still have girls falling at his feet. And that *voice*. It's... indescribable. Almost other-worldly. Every single note is like a sweet caress to the audience, despite the fact that he's not even singing a love song. I glance around the small theater and notice multiple girls, probably in their teens or early twenties, ogling him and giggling. Figures. I can't blame them, though. Even *I'm* nearly drooling. I feel heat rise to my cheeks as Skye nudges her arm with mine, a smile plastered on her face. Shit, I've been caught. I offer her a small smile and subtly cover my mouth with my hand, trying to hide the redness in my cheeks.

I glance at Skye on and off throughout the show and can't help but silently laugh at the pangs of jealousy that cross her face during particularly risqué scenes. Anyone who has ever been in a room with Skye and Aubrey can tell you there is absolutely *no way* Aubrey has eyes for anyone else, let alone a guy. I may not have been home much over the last month, but I've seen Aubrey over almost every single day and she is absolutely smitten.

Skye's jealousy is cute nevertheless. Meanwhile, I find myself jealous of Aubrey– what I wouldn't give to be under him like that...

Nope. Stop it.

This guy's girlfriend is probably somewhere in the audience just watching women like me pine over him. There is no way he's single, and even if by some miracle he were, it's not like I am in a place to do anything about it. James and I *just* broke up.

Then again a lot of guys would be down with being a rebound...

I subtly shake the thought from my head. What in the world has gotten into me?

When Sunshine and Aubrey reemerge from the wings, the crowd jumps to their feet in a standing ovation, myself included. As he smiles ear to ear in a bow, Sunshine's dimples pop through on each cheek. Just when I thought he couldn't be any cuter...

"What did you think?" Skye beams at me as the crowd starts shuffling for the exit.

"You were right, as usual. It was exactly what I needed and it was so good! Aubrey was *amazing*."

"What did you think of Sunshine?" She asks.

"He was great– very talented." I smile at her, trying to hide my sudden infatuation with this man that I don't even know.

The last thing I need is for Skye to figure out I'm even the least bit attracted to him. She's a great friend– the best I've ever had, hands down. But damn it, she's pushy. If I gave away anything, she'd never stop pushing me onto him. She wiggles her eyebrows before pulling me toward the backstage area.

"Aubrey!" She yells and runs over to her girlfriend, planting a huge kiss on her cheek. Aubrey scoops her up into a hug.

"Congratulations, Aubrey! It was phenomenal." I smile and give her a quick hug.

"Thanks Mia. I'm so happy you decided to come."

"Seriously babe, tonight was the best night of all of them. You *killed* it."

As Skye continues to sing her praises, I look around the backstage area, offering small smiles to multiple crew members cleaning up. I can't help but stare when my eyes land on Sunshine. I swear, he's even more gorgeous offstage. He's laughing with an older guy and a young girl as he fishes his mic out of his black, curly hair. He's not even looking at me and I can see how piercing his eyes are from here. He's still smiling when he glances in my direction, making eye contact. I pretend for a half-second like that smile is for me before I jerk my eyes back to Aubrey and Skye, hoping he didn't catch me staring.

"So you guys are coming, right?" Aubrey asks.

Damn, I missed more than half of the conversation.

"I'm sorry, where?" I ask.

"The party? For the cast and crew?" She's confused, so I assume she's already said this.

"Sorry babe, I made a deal with Mia that I'd get her back home straight away." Skye frowns momentarily but then gives a small, mischievous smile. "But we can drop you off there, right, Mi? I dropped her off earlier, so she doesn't have a car."

"Yeah, sure, of course." I smile at Aubrey before she gathers her things and heads for the door.

2

After a short car ride of Skye and me gushing to Aubrey about all of our favorite parts of the show, we pull up to a large house at the end of a quiet street on a cul-de-sac. Weird placement for a frat house if you ask me, but who am I to judge?

"Okay, so I'm going to pop inside for, like a quick eensy- weensy second, just to say hi to a few people. Do you want to come with me?" Skye says as she parks the car.

I look back at the beautiful house. There's a large tree in the front yard with a swing dangling from the leafless branches. People are sitting on a bench seat inside the large window at the front of the house and they look like they're having the time of their lives. Something about it feels so warm and inviting. I guess one minute wouldn't hurt.

"Yeah, sure." I nod. I swear there's a look exchanged between Aubrey and Skye before they giggle, but I don't catch it.

Once inside, Aubrey is nearly immediately ushered away by people singing her praises.

"There are drinks in the kitchen. I have to pee!" Skye shouts over the music.

She rushes off through the crowd in the direction of what I assume is the bathroom. Great. Now she's left me alone at a party that I didn't want to come to, in a house I've never been to before, where I don't know anyone. She's lucky I love her. I'm grateful for the house's has open concept and that the kitchen is near the entrance, otherwise I might have gotten lost. This place is downright gorgeous. There are really nice leather couches in the corner stuffed with guys playing video games on the large television over the brick fireplace. I catch a glimpse of the screen and they're playing some racing game, though you can't hear it because the music is *blaring*. The kitchen is just as impressive as the rest of the house. High ceilings, butcher block countertops on top of dark cabinets that line the walls and sit in the middle of the room with hanging lights overhead... I would *love* to cook in a kitchen this nice. It's almost a crime that there are pizza boxes stacked on the island. There's a punch bowl of blue liquid on the side of the boxes and I make my way toward it.

"You look absolutely miserable."

I had been so overwhelmed by the charm of the house, the sheer amount of people packed into it, and the volume of the music that I didn't even see Sunshine standing right next to me. I don't know why his presence surprises me. Of course he'd be here, he was in the cast. I fumble the ladle for the punch I'm trying to wrangle into two cups, but manage not to spill it. I'm not even one hundred percent sure what's in it but the smell is strong. I offer him a small smile, trying to hide whatever miserable look I must have had on my face.

"Oh, hi! Not miserable, just not supposed to be here. And it's so loud! Why are college parties always so loud?"

He laughs, and my god those dimples...

"Something about a rite of passage, I would guess."

"You were amazing tonight." I set the cups on the table in front of me and stretch out a hand. "I'm Mia."

His hand is much bigger than mine as he shakes it. His grip is friendly but firm and he lingers there for a moment.

"Sunshine."

I laugh again internally at the ridiculousness of his name. I'm about to say I noticed that in the program, but he continues.

"My mom was... a bit of a hippie, but I've learned to like it. Most of my friends just call me by my last name, Parker."

"It's definitely unique!" I can't help but smile at him and try, but fail, to stop the small laugh that emerges.

Way to go, Mia. Laugh at his name right to his face, why don't you?

When he flashes a smile at me, I swear my knees go weak. I internally curse at them to stop because I don't have time to get distracted by his cute dimples. I shouldn't even be talking to him. I literally just broke off a three-year engagement and I *have* to focus on school if I want to finish somewhat on time.

"Well," I say, picking up my red solo cups from the table. "I better get back to my friend."

He gently lays a hand on my elbow before I can make a clean getaway, the feeling of his hand on me sending goosebumps down my arms.

"Wait up. Have we met before? I know almost everyone here, and you look so familiar, but I can't place it..."

I shrug and shake my head. "I just transferred here."

I have to yell for him to hear me over the music, which has somehow gotten even louder. I feel someone bump into my back, causing me to stumble forward slightly and let out a breath of frustration.

"Do you want to go sit outside or something? There's a deck out back and it's not as loud."

He points his thumb over his shoulder at a set of French doors. Everything in me is screaming that this is a bad idea. I don't know him, and I only have enough bandwidth for school right now– but who could resist that voice? He's like a magnet and I can't resist his pull. I don't think I've ever been this attracted to anyone in my life.

"Don't you have admirers that need to tell you how amazing you were tonight?"

The corner of his mouth lifts in a gorgeous, mischievous grin.

"Oh sorry, was that not what you were planning on doing? You know actors can't go more than five minutes without praise, right? Legend has it our heads spontaneously combust."

"I'll make sure I really stroke your ego, then." I laugh.

I scan the crowd for Skye and find her in the corner of the room watching some others play a round of beer pong as she whispers something in Aubrey's ear, causing her to giggle.

"I'll meet you out there." I smile at him and head for Skye.

"Did you decide we're staying?" She shouts as I hand over her drink.

"Yeah, it's fine, we can hang out for a bit. It's just really loud in here."

She taps the side of my cup with hers in a toast. "Thanks, Sweets."

"I'm going to head outside to actually hear myself think."

"Do you want me to come with you?" Skye asks, pushing herself upright from the wall she'd been leaning on.

"No, no. Have fun. It's cool." I shake my head, before stifling a smile and heading toward the doors Sunshine left through.

The partially-covered rear deck is attached to a covered in-ground pool with fairy lights strung up overhead. The jacuzzi off to the side of the pool is occupied by a few people, beers in hand and enthralled in conversation. Over in the yard there are some people gathered around a brick bonfire and in the corner of the yard there's a small, frozen over pond. This is unlike any frat house I went to at Duke. Aren't they usually supposed to be chaotic and unkempt? There's not too many people on the deck, but those who are seem to be coupled up, standing around the pool and drinking. I find Sunshine isolated from the others on one of the lounge chairs to the left of the pool, wearing a large coat and a beanie. How is it possible that he has the ability to turn the quiet act of phone-scrolling into something so effortlessly enchanting?

"Hey," I say, grateful to finally be able to speak at a normal volume despite the pounding bass filtering through to outside.

He looks up with a smile, pocketing his phone, and pats the spot next to him. I cross my arms to close my coat fully before taking a seat next to him. It's so cold we can see our breath, but I feel inexplicably warm. It's got to be the alcohol.

"So I'm guessing parties aren't your thing?"

"Definitely not," I say. "My friend said she just wanted to say hi to a few people, but I figured we could stay for a bit."

"Who's your friend?" He asks, taking a long pull of the beer bottle in his hand.

"Skye? Skye Jensen?"

Sunshine nearly spits his beer out when I say her name.

"Oh shit, you're *that* Mia! How did I not put it together before? That's why I recognized you! Skye's got pictures of you *everywhere* at her place. You're all she's talked about for months. I swear I feel like I already know you."

Anxiety prickles at my neck as I think of what Skye may have divulged. How much of my damage does he already know thanks to Skye? I offer him a small smile and stay silent, unsure what to say .

"Parties aren't really my thing either," he says, after what feels like too many minutes of silence. "I wouldn't be here if I didn't have to, honestly. Kind of unavoidable though."

"I mean, I guess, but just because you're talented doesn't mean you have to do what everyone else wants you to. I'd bet after that performance you just want to cuddle up in your bed and sleep."

"Well yeah, but it would be kind of loud," he says, gesturing to the party, and it finally clicks.

"Wait, you live here?"

"Yeah, me and my two roommates."

"I thought it was some kind of frat house... Until I saw the inside at least. This house is gorgeous," I say.

Sunshine's eyes crinkle when he laughs and it's so adorable I worry I may *actually* swoon.

"Thanks. We mostly just sit around and play video games in our downtime, though." He shrugs. "We really only have cast parties here."

"Wouldn't you rather your house not get trashed?"

"Well yeah, of course, but I also don't like the idea of people drinking and driving. We have the space to let people stay if they need to. They just have to help clean in the morning."

I raise my cup to him. "The best hangover cure."

He clinks the side of his beer bottle with my cup.

"So you said you transferred? How come?" He asks.

Relief floods me at the realization that he must not know much.

"It's a long story."

"Well lucky for you, I've got nothing but time."

His whole body is turned toward me, waiting for me to continue. His beautiful blue eyes are kind and slightly squinted from the soft, encouraging smile he's wearing. His cheeks are red from the cold and I want nothing more than to put my hands over them to warm them.

"Shouldn't you be socializing?"

"I am."

"I feel guilty taking the star away from the party."

"Nah, don't. There will be plenty more cast parties. Plus, I'm enjoying myself."

The heat that floods my cheeks probably makes them match his. I can only hope he assumes it's also from the cold.

"Well, let's see... I was studying Biology at Duke so I could get into a good med program when I-"

"Wait, like Duke, Duke?" He interjects.

The surprise he wears is so evident I'm almost offended.

"Yep, that's the one."

"Wow. So why the hell did you transfer to Eastview? Why *Iowa*?" He asks, wrinkling his nose in disgust.

"Well, I was getting there before you *rudely* cut me off," I jest, nudging his elbow with mine. "Anyway, I realized that I didn't actually want to be a doctor... It probably took me longer than it should have, but I knew my mom would get upset if I actually admitted it."

"Ahh, the parental guilt trip."

"It was a little more than that. Mom's wanted me to go to Duke since I was like, I don't know, five? She had a whole plan. I had perfect attendance, I was enrolled in all AP classes... Hell, I even skipped third grade... I mean, clearly she knew what she was doing because it all worked. I wound up getting a full ride. I just..." I shake my head. "I couldn't do it."

"So does your mom live nearby then?"

"Somewhat, yeah. I grew up near Davenport. But honestly, I missed my brother more than my mom."

"Wait, so you said you skipped a grade... How old are you then?"

"Twenty. But I'm *almost* twenty-one."

"Ooookay," he says, gently taking my drink out of my hand.

My mouth drops open in shock as he tosses the contents into the nearby grass and puts my cup on the ground. Rude.

"Sorry, I just don't want any trouble. If the cops were to show up or something, I'd be the one getting arrested. Typically we kick people out when they drink underage."

"So... are you going to kick me out?" I ask.

"And miss the chance to get to know the famous Mia? No way. Just cutting you off."

"Fine, so how old are you then? What year are you?" I cross my arms.

I'm still slightly disappointed that I won't get to finish my drink, but the tingling feeling shooting down my legs indicates that it was probably a bit too strong and I would've cut myself off shortly anyways. If past experiences are any indicator, Skye will definitely be in no condition to drive and the last thing I can do is stay the night here.

"Twenty two. I guess I'm technically a senior but I've also changed majors a time or two, so I still have a year left."

"Lucky you. Between my bachelor's and grad school it feels like I'll never be done." I sigh and rub my hands up and down my thighs, trying to simultaneously get rid of the tingling and also warm them up. The wind picks up and suddenly I'm keenly aware of just how *cold* it is.

"I'm going to pop inside really quickly, okay? Don't go anywhere." Sunshine stands and heads for the sliding door.

Well that was... abrupt. I exhale a long, hot breath into my hands once he's inside and pull my hood over my head. I turn to sit properly on the lounge chair and curl my legs upward, trying to gather any body heat I can. I'm half-tempted to follow Sunshine inside when he emerges through the sliding glass door with his hands full.

"You looked cold," he says as he slides another lounge chair close to mine and hands me a blanket and hoodie. "I brought you hot chocolate and water, too. I wasn't sure what you'd want."

"Oh my gosh, thank you so much." I smile at him and stand, the heat returning to my cheeks.

I hurry out of my coat and into the hoodie before sliding the coat back on and wrapping myself up in the blanket. Sunshine puts the hot chocolate and a water bottle he had put in his pocket on the ground beside my chair, and sits on the edge of his.

"We can go inside if you want? Or sit by the fire?" He suggests.

"No, I'm okay, now." I glance over at the group of people near the fire who are laughing loudly and nudging each other. "You can go though if you want to, I don't want to keep you."

"Okay, bye." Sunshine starts to stand but then lays back on the lounge chair, a big smile on his face as he turns to look at me.

I giggle and curl my body tighter, turning on my side to face him.

"So grad school, huh?" he asks. "I couldn't do it. The sooner I'm done with school, the better."

"Well, I changed my major to education, so I've got two more years here, then student teaching, and then *maybe* grad school, but who knows."

"Mia, I mean this in the nicest way possible, but are you a masochist? Because that sounds like literal torture."

"Okay Mister Too Cool for School, what's your goal after graduation?" I feign offense.

"Broadway, obviously," he says sarcastically, with a wave of his hand.

"I could see it. You're insanely talented."

He silently stares at me for a moment before his face breaks into a cocky smile.

"What?" I laugh.

"I'm just glad we've finally arrived at the stroking– I mean, ego-stroking– portion of the evening."

He winks at me and I can't stop laughing. His eyes twinkle at me while he wears a giant grin and his shoulders shake in a silent laugh, which only makes me laugh more.

Getting to know Sunshine is like taking a deep breath of the crispest, purest air– refreshing, invigorating, and a little addictive. He's effortlessly funny, endlessly kind, and if I haven't made it clear enough yet... he's hot as hell. A few curls peek out from underneath his beanie and I can't stop staring into his eyes, hoping I'm not coming off as creepy. They're just so beautiful. Mostly blue with a light gold starburst of color near his pupils and a darker shade blue lining the outside all hidden behind long, dark lashes...

"Hey Mi?" Skye's voice interrupts my thoughts as she emerges through the sliding door, looking around until her eyes land on me and she breaks into a smile. "Oh, hey Parker."

She's thrown her voice up a few octaves when she addresses Sunshine, as if we just got caught doing something we shouldn't.

"Jensen!" Sunshine exclaims, throwing an arm around Skye in a hug when she approaches.

Skye returns his hug before she squats down in front of me so we're eye level and speaks in a muttered voice.

"I just wanted to check on you and see how you're doing out here, but it seems as though someone has beat me to it."

She raises her eyebrows at me suggestively.

"I see you've met Mia." Skye turns to Sunshine. "I told you she was gorgeous."

I avert my gaze to avoid seeing his reaction at her awkward outburst. I wish I could say I was surprised by it, but at this point I know better than to expect Skye to filter herself. When she turns her attention back to me, I roll my eyes and she pats my leg.

"Listen, it's getting late and I know you wanted to get to bed at a decent hour. You wanna get going?"

I glance down at my phone for the time. Damn. It's midnight already, and I'm internally cursing at myself for scheduling an eight AM class on Mondays. How did the time move so quickly?

"Ah shit," I sigh. "Yeah, we probably should."

"It's been great talking with you." Sunshine smiles at me and stands up.

I smile back at him and nod while he takes in Skye's red, glossy eyes.

"Are you okay to drive, Jensen?"

"Yeah," she throws a hand up to shoo him off with a wave, trying to be nonchalant but giving off anything but sober vibes.

"I'll drive." I say, taking her keys from her and feeling grateful that Sunshine decorated his lawn with my drink.

Sunshine hugs Skye and I watch as his muscles flex when he does. Man, that looks like a good hug. I tug at the sleeve on my coat to give Sunshine his hoodie back.

"No, it's okay– you hold onto it. If you take your coat off again, you'll be freezing. Are you a hugger?" he asks and I nod.

He wraps his arms around me and *holy shit* he smells good. Like cedarwood, and beer, and citrus, and something I can't quite place. It takes everything in me to not be a creep and inhale his scent. His hug is tight, but not overbearing, and I have a hard time making myself break away from it.

"You smell nice," he whispers in my ear, echoing my own thoughts, as he pulls away from me. The absence of his arms makes me cold again, but I feel my cheeks heat up as I offer him a small smile. "Jensen, let me know when you get home."

Skye nods and puts her arm in mine. She waits until we're nearly to the car, where Aubrey is waiting, before she whispers.

"Okay, you have to tell me *everything*."

I give minor details of my conversation with Sunshine as we make the drive to drop Aubrey off at her apartment, trying to keep it as basic as possible. I hate having to filter myself, especially with Skye, but I really don't want her to push anything. She would though, even if unintentionally. When I park, I watch as Skye gets out and rounds the car, pulling Aubrey into a long embrace. I hug my arms to my chest. Fuck, I miss being held.

There's a very tiny part of me that still misses James. I definitely don't want to get back together with him or anything, but he went from being one of my best friends to my boyfriend to my fiancé to just not being in my life at all. It's been six months and I haven't even heard from him once. He wouldn't even acknowledge my existence in class after everything went down. I knew I had hurt him despite my best effort to let him down gently, but I never expected for it to blow up so many aspects of my life so spectacularly. Sometimes I wish I could take it all back, if only so I could feel less alone. Other times I wish we'd never crossed over from friends to more at all. I quickly blink away the tears threatening to fall as Skye gets back in the car and cranks the radio.

I hang Skye's keys on the hook near the door as she heads to the kitchen counter, popping a few ibuprofen to prevent the inevitable hangover that she'll have tomorrow.

"So Sunshine, huh?" She nudges me once she's taken a seat next to me on the couch.

"What about him?" I ask as casually as I can.

"You're going to go for it, right? He's such a freaking sweetheart. If I were into guys, I wouldn't even hesitate." She pauses, looking down at her phone and typing. "I'm telling you Mi, he's one of the good ones."

One of the good ones. I've heard that before. It's the same thing I've heard about James my entire life from everyone *except* Skye, and look how that turned out.

"I'm sure he is," I sigh, standing. "Anyway, I have to go to bed. We'll talk more tomorrow. I'll be gone most of the day, but I should be home for dinner."

"Remember that you're supposed to have *fun* in college too!" She shouts as I walk off to my room. I flip her off and my phone chirps with an incoming text from a local number.

> Glad to hear you're home safe. Have a great first day tomorrow, Mia. I really hope you like it here.

You know those old cartoons where the character's heart beats so hard it pops out of their chest and you can see the outline, while their eyes are replaced with little hearts? I swear if I didn't know that was physically impossible, that would be me right now.

"Did you give my number to Sunshine?!" I shout from my room.

"You're welcome!"

I look back down at my phone and can't help the giant, goofy smile that takes over my face as I type back a response.

> Thanks Sunshine. Night!

I take a steadying breath and remind myself that I *just* met this guy. He doesn't even know me and I am in no way, shape or form, ready for another relationship. I can only hope that he and Skye aren't too close so she doesn't have many opportunities for meddling.

I put my headphones in and turn on my bedtime playlist, jam packed full of slow hits anywhere from the sixties to today. The Beatles' soft melody plays through my headphones and I close my eyes, slipping Sunshine's hoodie over my nose and inhaling.

3

I toss and turn all night before fully waking up ahead of my alarm. First days have always made me nervous and my stomach is in knots. I sigh and rub my eyes, knowing I'm not going to be able to go back to sleep. I guess this is as good a time as any to start getting myself together. Skye doesn't have classes until later so I try to be quiet as I heat up a quick breakfast. I can't stop thinking about last night. Sunshine's soft hand as he shook mine... his smile... his kind eyes... and that hug...If *Skye*—the ultimate man-hater, fight-the-patriarchy, woman-power type—says he's one of the good ones, he must be, right? Not that it matters anyways. It *can't* matter. I'm far too much of a mess for anyone to want to get sucked into. The coffee pot's three short beeps pull me from my thoughts and I pour some in a travel mug before pouring some cream and lots of sugar into it. I take the last bite of my toast, before grabbing my backpack, keys, and coat. It's freezing and I'm already dying for it to be summer again, but even with the fresh coat of snow on the ground I finally have a sense of belonging. I only wish I had visited Skye here all the times she invited me, then maybe I'd have made the move sooner.

Between my two classes this morning and a short, three hour shift at the library, I'm exhausted when I finally stumble into my last class of the day. It's finally the class I'm most excited about— Introduction to American Sign Language. Not only does it fulfill a language requirement, but I've always found the language and Deaf culture to be fascinating. Hopefully I'll be able to use it at least once in my career.

I plop down into my chair and take a breath, tired from the trek uphill. The lack of sleep from last night is catching up to me and I rub my eyes again before taking my headphones out of my ears.

"Oh hey, Mia. I'm glad to see we have a class together." Sunshine takes the seat next to me. He's hanging his coat on the back of his chair and wearing his beanie with his curls poking out from underneath.

Of course I have a class with Sunshine. Why wouldn't I have a class with Sunshine? The universe loves to torture me, after all. I sit up straighter and run my hands over my hair. Why the hell didn't I wear any makeup today?

"Oh hey! Same... it is surprising though, this campus is huge."

"Listen, if you can handle *Duke,* you can handle Eastview. What classes are you taking?" he asks, and I watch as his eyes widen when I hand him my class schedule. "Woah. So you're basically going to be living at the library, huh?"

"Yeah, I guess it's a good thing I work there, too."

"Damn," he says and I shrug.

"I had to take out quite a bit of student loans to come here... I don't want to be here longer than I have to."

Professor Strieber welcomes the class, so we both face forward. My phone chimes out loud and I quickly move to silence it, my cheeks turning red at the face Professor Strieber gives me before she reminds everyone to silence their phones. I glance down and see a text from Sunshine waiting.

> I can help you with ASL if you want

I glance over at him and he is still facing forward, an amused, cocky smile playing on the corner of his lips.

> Oh yeah? You think you'll be better at it than me huh?

> Something like that

> I need to pay attention so I can help YOU. Stop distracting me. :P

I glance over at him again and see his chest move in a silent laugh before he types back.

> Distracting you? You're the one with the phone going off in the middle of class Mia. ;)

I laugh under my breath and tuck my phone back in my pocket. I'm trying so hard to pay attention, but I'm too aware of Sunshine next to me. I sneak a look at him again, trying not to be obvious. He's sitting back, holding a pencil and rocking it back and forth between his fingers. His other arm is draped across his thigh lazily. He looks so relaxed and carefree that it reminds me to take a deep breath, feeling some hidden tension leave my body as I do. I wish I could be so effortlessly calm on the first day.

When class is dismissed, I offer Sunshine a small smile and a wave before making my way out the door. Of course I wanted to talk to him, but what the hell do I even say after I was practically drooling over him last night? I'm simultaneously relieved and disappointed when he doesn't try to catch up with me.

When I walk through the door of the apartment, I hang my coat and keys on the hooks near the door before slumping into a chair at the kitchen table, putting my head down. The large windows in the living room have the curtains drawn, letting in a lot of natural light and the delicious aroma of Skye's famous Chicken Spaghetti is in the air.

"Long day?" She asks.

"Yeah, I had to meet with my advisor after my last class and then I got stuck behind a train on my way home... I'm exhausted and starving."

"Well lucky for you, dinner will be ready soon. I invited someone over for dinner tonight, hope you don't mind."

"Aubrey?" I ask, confused, and she shakes her head, "Who?"

"It's just this guy I know." She waves me off.

"You're joking, right? I've had the longest day and you're inviting random guys over?" I groan.

"Ouch, Mia. Is that all I am to you? A random guy?" Sunshine is all smiles as he comes out of the bathroom, hand on his chest feigning offense.

He's taken his hat off, letting his curls roam free, and the mere sight of him gives me butterflies. Nearly everything in me tells me to stay away, but there's still that small part of me that wants to run over, jump into his arms, run my hands in his hair, and kiss him. Okay, maybe a large part of me.

"Oh, hey, sorry. I didn't realize it was you... I've just had a really long day."

"I get it, I was just joking. I take it Skye didn't tell you she invited me over for dinner," he laughs, running a hand through his curls.

"Oh, no she didn't, but you're welcome to stay of course." I give him a small smile and sit up straighter in my chair.

When Skye finishes loading three plates with food, Sunshine and I each grab a plate and retreat to the table with Skye following close behind.

"How were classes?" Skye asks, though I'm not quite sure who she's asking.

"Fine." I nod.

"Mia and I are in ASL together."

"I thought you were joking when you said you were taking that!" Skye laughs and turns to me. "Did he tell you he's already fluent?"

"Uh, nope. He didn't mention that." I say, starting to eat.

"I was ceasing my distraction as requested," he teases. "My little sister was born Deaf so the whole family pretty much knows sign. I'm just taking it to fulfill a language requirement... seemed like an easy A." He says and takes a bite, groaning in satisfaction.

"So you two are friends, I take it?" I ask, gesturing between Skye and Sunshine with my fork.

"Yeah, we met when he first tried to steal my girlfriend freshman year and now we tolerate each other." Skye teases.

"Okay, wait, we've been over this. I've never tried to steal your girlfriend. Just because we *play* love interests doesn't mean I'm *interested* in her."

"Well forgive *me* but you guys seem to play love interests *a lot*," she laughs.

"We can't help that we're talented," he says with a shrug. "Where is she anyway?"

"She has late classes on Mondays. I'll probably pop by her place after dinner."

As I watch their interaction, I realize that they more than tolerate each other. I get the feeling that Sunshine is a regular at our apartment because that would be just my luck. All I know is if he's going to be here a lot, I'm going to need this little crush to fuck right off. I can't be making googly eyes at him all the damn time when I need to focus on school and school alone.

"So why did *you* decide to take ASL, Mia?" Sunshine asks, turning to me.

"I don't know," I say. "I've always been fascinated with the language and the culture, I guess. I also think about Deaf kids who are put in hearing schools... I guess I'd just like to be able to communicate with them, at least a little bit, without an interpreter."

"That's amazing. My sister would love you."

"How old is she?" I ask.

"She's ten." He smiles.

"Oh I forgot how close she is in age to Frankie! Did Mia tell you she has a totes adorbs eleven-year-old brother?" Skye interjects.

"Yeah," he nods. "She mentioned that. Not the... totes adorbs part though."

"You guys have *so* much in common." Skye beams before standing. "Well, I'm going to head to Aubrey's. Don't wait up. You guys can handle the dishes, right?"

I nod. "Thanks for dinner Skye."

She kisses both our cheeks and practically skips out the door.

"Well she couldn't have been more obvious, could she?" Sunshine laughs after a beat of silence.

I feel the heat on my cheeks and put my face in my hands.

"Sorry," I say, unbelievably flustered. "She can be a bit much– she's always been like that so I'm just kind of used to it."

"How long have you been friends?"

"I've basically known her since I was born. Our moms were best friends, so we were too."

There's an awkward silence as I try to find things to talk about. Even just sitting and eating I'm mesmerized by him. I take a small but audible breath to try to steady my heartbeat.

"She loves you, you know. Anyone who knows Skye has heard about you and how great you are since freshman year."

"She probably oversold me." I laugh.

"Nah, I don't think so."

I wish I could read his mind with the way he's smiling at me. Does he feel this electric current running through him like I do? Does he feel the same pull?

"Did she say anything about why I transferred?"

I don't know what possessed me to ask it and I'm not even sure I want to know the answer. No matter what, it seems my past will continue to haunt me. He seems to think a moment before looking up from his food and responding.

"She mentioned that you were in a relationship and it didn't work out, and that you wanted to move closer to home."

I nod awkwardly. Awesome. He knows about James. I try to reassure myself that this is for the best— surely he won't pursue me knowing I was recently engaged— but the sinking feeling of disappointment that he won't is harder to ignore.

"We can talk about it if you want," he offers.

He's finished eating and he's sitting with his body facing mine again. I'm not sure if I want him to know the whole story yet, but when I look at him his eyes are warm and kind. Everything about this man is inviting, so it's hard not to be distracted by his presence alone.

"He was my first boyfriend," I say after a beat, "We started dating like freshman year of high school, I think? I've known him since I was a kid and our parents were friends. He asked me to marry him when I was 16 and he was 18. My mom absolutely *loved* him and I think she would've given her permission to marry him the second he asked, but I wanted to finish college first. By some miracle, we both got into Duke... I just couldn't go through with it."

"What happened?" He asks, gathering my empty plate and heading to the sink. I follow. "I'll wash, you dry?"

"Sure. And I don't know, honestly. It's... hard to explain I guess. I think it was probably for the best that we had stayed friends to begin with." I dry dishes as he hands them to me.

"Damn, engaged and then friend-zoned," he laughs.

"Yeah... I don't think we're friends so much anymore. He kind of hates me... and understandably so. It wasn't exactly fair to him. Here he thought everything was totally fine. I think I was so focused on making sure he was happy and my mom was happy that I didn't make sure I was. I thought how I was feeling was normal since I'd known him so long, you know?" I shrug. "I don't know. It wasn't really until Skye met Aubrey and I heard the way she talked about her that I realized I wanted that too someday."

"So what was the tipping point? Why did you decide to leave?" He asks.

The day I ended things with James is a day that I deliberately try to avoid thinking about. I debate the answer for a moment, unsure of what to say. My cheeks are hot with embarrassment already and I haven't even said anything. As if sensing my discomfort, he speaks up again.

"Sorry, you don't have to tell me if you don't want to."

"We wanted different things," I say, choosing my words carefully.

"Yeah I guess that would make it difficult. You deserve to be with some-one who can give you what you want."

I watch as he continues to wash the dishes and dry them as he hands them to me. I'm conflicted because while a part of me feels very awkward, I also feel very comfortable. We wash and dry the dishes side by side and I feel my stomach do a flip when his hand occasionally grazes mine while handing me a dish.

"Why do you care?" I ask tentatively, and he shrugs.

"Any friend of Skye is a friend of mine, so I figured we're friends now." He smiles at me.

"And I get no say in this?" I laugh.

"Nope, you're stuck with me now."

"Well I guess if I'm stuck with you, you can help me pass my classes and get through this semester." I nudge him with my elbow, desperately trying to change the subject.

"Sounds like a lot of work, but I can probably do that." He flicks some water at me, playfully. "After we're done we can get to your first signing lesson."

"Oh wait! I think I already know one!" I throw up my middle finger, smiling sweetly, and he laughs, drying his hands off on a nearby towel and turning to stand in front of me.

"Well yeah, most people do. Here, this is friends." He signs the word friends to me and I copy it. Then he signs something to me and I don't catch anything other than the word "friend." When I give him a confused look he just lets out a small laugh and heads for the couch, where I follow.

Sunshine signs with such ease as he teaches me several words I ask about, and I am in awe. This man knows a whole other *language*. I know a little bit of Spanish after taking it for four years, but ASL is so much more beautiful. Every once in a while I get caught up on a sign and he moves my hands with his, every touch making my heart race. Is that on purpose? I even occasionally catch myself staring at his lips while he talks, wondering what they taste like. What the hell is wrong with me? I feel obsessed, and it's kind of freaking me out. I run my hands over my face, feeling the pull of exhaustion, and glance down at my phone to check the time. How in the world is it one a.m. already? Between the ASL lesson and learning more about each other, the time flew by and now I don't want him to leave. I can't remember the last time I met someone I could talk to for hours.

"Shit, it's late." I sigh and he checks his phone for the time as well.

"Oh yeah, I better head out." he stretches out and lets out a yawn.

"Are you going to be okay driving?" I ask, concern lacing my voice far more than I want it to.

"Yeah." He rubs his eyes and blinks them a few times. "I'll blast music or something."

"You can crash on the couch if you want..." I try not to sound too hopeful.

"Are you sure?" He raises an eyebrow.

"Yeah, I wouldn't be able to forgive myself if something happened to you because you dozed off."

"Yeah, okay."

I head to the linen closet to grab an extra blanket and pillow for him and hold them out to him.

"Goodnight, Mia. Thank you," he says, moving closer to me, his blue eyes piercing through my heart.

He leans his body closer to mine and my breath hitches in anticipation before he smiles and gives me a hug. Of course he wasn't going to kiss me, he doesn't even know me.

"You're welcome," I say, blushing in embarrassment and then move quickly to my room.

I lay in my bed, staring at the ceiling. I can almost still feel his hands on mine. I swear it's like every time he's around I'm either blushing like crazy or just staring at him like a weirdo. I'm an idiot. There's something about being around him though. It's like he's the sun and I'm being sucked into orbit. I know I can't; it wouldn't be fair to him... There's nothing wrong with dreaming about it though, right?

4

Thoughts of having Sunshine in the apartment just a few feet from my room wakes me up way earlier than I prefer, so I decide to make breakfast. I didn't hear Skye come in last night, and her empty room leaves me to assume that she stayed the night at Aubrey's place. When I walk by the couch, I hesitate at the end when I see Sunshine sleeping soundly. His hair is disheveled and his alluring blue eyes are peacefully closed. He slept without a shirt on and he's asleep on his stomach. His body is well-sculpted and I'm back to practically drooling. I notice a tattoo on his shoulder that looks like it extends to his chest but I can't quite make out what it is without getting too close. I take a few quiet steps closer to look at it, but quickly make my escape to the kitchen when he turns to his side in his sleep. I move about as quietly as possible to avoid waking him and start a pot of coffee. I'm ladling the pancakes into the pan when I hear the front door open. Oh fuck.

"Oh hey Mi, you're up ear-" I hear Skye start and then gesture for her to be quiet and point to a sleeping Sunshine on the couch.

"Oh. My. God," she whispers and rushes to me in the kitchen with a huge smile on her face. "Tell me everything!"

"We were just hanging out and talking and we lost track of time. That's all. I figured you wouldn't care since you guys seem to be friends," I whisper back and she gives me a skeptical look, causing me to raise my hands in defense. "I swear that's it. He was helping me study."

"You are *so* crushing on him. And I don't blame you. The man is gorgeous."

"It doesn't matter," I shake my head. Clearly trying to hide it from Skye is pointless.

"And why is that?" She asks and puts her hands on her hips. "You're making breakfast for the guy for crying out loud."

"I'm making breakfast for *all* of us. And you know why. It wouldn't be fair to him. I have to focus on school. I haven't even been home to visit Frankie yet. Not to mention, I was *just* engaged to *marry* someone else not that long ago. It's too soon."

"Ok first off, clearly you've made time for something other than school." She gestures to the couch. "Second, Frankie knows you love him and do you *really* wanna go home with your mom being as pissed as she is?"

I shake my head no quickly. I'm avoiding taking that bullet for as long as I possibly can.

"And third, it's been four months, Mia. It's not like you're not over that relationship because you were never *into* it. Clearly you're into Sunshine and he's *definitely* into you," she gushes.

"What? No. No, he isn't. And even if he were, it doesn't matter, Skye. I don't know *what* I want. I ruined a lot of friendships because I *thought* I loved James, but I didn't. If Sunshine is going to be in my life, it'll be as friends. That's what I can handle right now." I finish the pancakes and start on the eggs.

"Okay, okay," she puts her hands up in surrender, "I just don't want to see him get snatched up by another girl. He would be so good for you."

"I just met him," I argue. "He doesn't even know me."

"And imagine how much more he's going to want you once he does." She says and moves to sit at the table.

"Hardly." I give a small, sarcastic laugh.

We hear a yawn and turn to see arms stretch above the couch.

"What smells so good?" Sunshine stands up, his voice gravelly and clipped as he stretches.

I have to force myself to keep my cool, because holy shit this man without a shirt! I shift my legs uncomfortably and try to ignore the urge to nuzzle myself into his chest. Skye lets out a small laugh and then whistles a cat call. Sunshine laughs, gives a small bow, and puts a shirt on.

"I made breakfast." I smile at him, my nerves still on edge.

"Awesome! Jensen, you didn't tell me she could also cook!" He exclaims.

"That's because I was too busy cooking for you instead." She sticks her tongue out at him while I plate the food.

"Here let me help you," he says and grabs plates to put on the table, smiling down at me as he takes them.

"So what's your schedule today Mi?" Skye asks and we all start eating.

"I actually don't have that many classes today. I should be home around three." I respond between bites.

"Do you want more help with ASL today? I get done around five and can swing by after?" Sunshine suggests.

"I really appreciate it but I was going to go through the syllabuses for my classes and mark some deadlines in my planner."

"Oh, that's so boring, Mi. Maybe Sunshine can help make sure you don't miss any deadlines? Or maybe he can help you finally unpack those boxes in your room."

I freeze in my seat at the mention of the boxes.

"Lay off her Skye," Sunshine laughs, and stands up to bring his plate to the sink. "Thank you for breakfast, Mia. I'll see you in English."

"Wait, what?" I ask.

"I saw it on your schedule yesterday. We're in the same comp class." He gives Skye a hug as he speaks and walks over to me as well.

"Oh, sweet. I guess I'll see you later then." I say, standing, and he pulls me into a big hug. He is such a good hugger, and he smells amazing. How does someone who just woke up smell this good?

I look at Skye and she's giving me a knowing look after Sunshine heads out the door, closing it behind him. I roll my eyes at her before heading to my room to get ready before facing the day ahead.

The day *drags* as I find myself looking forward to comp class... and hating myself for looking forward to it. This just isn't me. I've never been the type of girl that goes gaga over a guy after a few meetings. Not even once James started showing interest in me did I let him infiltrate my mind the way Sunshine has been. I've always been the kind of girl that focuses on her goals first, letting any romantic interests take a backseat. Then again, I've only ever been in one relationship... Now here I am almost giddy as I take a seat in the front row in comp class in hopes to be able to pay attention.

"Fancy running into you here." Sunshine arrives a few minutes later and takes the seat next to me.

"You know, if I didn't know any better, I'd think you're stalking me." I tease.

"Maybe I am, maybe I'm not, you'll never know." He wiggles his eyebrows at me mischievously.

I try to force myself to focus while the professor speaks, but his desk is way too close to mine. When did I become the type of person that gets distracted by the mere proximity of someone else? After class, Sunshine softly grabs my elbow as I pack up my backpack.

"You're headed to the humanities building, right?" He asks.

"What, did you like, memorize my schedule? Should I be worried, stalker?"

"No," he laughs "Nothing like that. I was trying to see what classes I could help you with since clearly you're going to be driving yourself crazy this semester. It's on my way to my next class, so I thought we could walk together."

The walk towards the humanities building is quiet as Sunshine walks beside me, his arm occasionally brushing against mine. Despite the fact that there are several layers or fabric between us, my body still decides to adorn itself with a plethora of goosebumps. Luckily goosebumps on the face aren't a thing, or I'd be really embarrassed right now.

"How are you liking Eastview?" He asks.

"It's great." I smile. "I love the campus. It's so beautiful."

"Just wait until the Fall. All of the leaves change, the air is somehow cleaner and like, more refreshing... It's the best time for picnics."

I smile at him, unsure what to say. It seems I can either divulge way too much information or give him shit... with not a lot in between. If we're going to be friends, I need to be able to have an actual conversation with him without pining after him. We walk in silence for a few more minutes. As we walk, there are plenty of girls that either smile as he walks past them or seem bashful in his presence. I'm glad I'm not the only one he has an effect on.

"So I have to come clean about something," he says, turning to walk backward so he's facing me.

"Go on..."

"I think I heard you and Skye talking and I swore it was just a dream but then I saw that you two were actually talking when I woke up... Were you guys talking about me this morning?" He asks.

Fuck. Fuck a duck. I've known this guy for just a few days. Now I have to tell him like *hey I know I'm being presumptuous but I don't want to date you.* And not even like I don't *want* to. I mean come on, he's *gorgeous.* But not only that, he's also incredibly sweet and actually listens when I talk like it's the most interesting thing he's ever heard... it's freezing outside but my cheeks are on fire. It's been too long since I've said anything and he's looking at me expectantly with a hint of a smile.

"Ok, yeah, we were, but I don't want you to think I'm being forward or anything. I mean we just met each other and we barely know each other but Skye is being really adamant that-"

I stop talking when he starts laughing. Oh, kill me now. Of course he doesn't want to date me. I would love nothing more than to go die in a hole at this moment.

"You're cute when you're nervous," he says. "It's cool, I heard you. If friends are what you need, then a friend is what I'll be."

"It's just... I'm kind of a mess right now and you don't even know me," I nearly whisper.

It isn't until Sunshine stops in front of me and grabs my hand, removing it from my face that I realize I'm biting my nails, a nasty habit I've had since I was a kid. Most of the time I don't even realize I'm doing it. I'm dying for him to keep hold of my hand when he lets it go.

"I want to though."

If we have any real chance of being friends, I need to shut this down. He deserves the truth and I can't handle this awkward, sheepish feeling that I get whenever he's around.

"Here's the thing," I start, ignoring the way my heart flutters at the way his hand feels against mine, "I feel something for you, but I don't know what *it* is. I thought that what I felt for James was love, but it wasn't and it broke him when we broke up. He won't even talk to me and he used to be one of my closest friends. A lot of my other friends took his side of things too. I couldn't let that happen with you. I don't want to hurt you, and you're friends with Skye and Aubrey. They're literally my only friends right now and that's just because they didn't like James. They love you."

"Well first of all, there isn't a scenario short of you murdering me where Skye takes my side of anything over yours. Do you realize the way she talks about you? When she said you were enrolling here, I was so stoked. And not only because I thought you were beautiful in the millions of pictures she has of you guys, but because she spoke so highly of you."

"She's my best friend, of course she's only going to tell you the good things," I say and look back down at my shoes.

"What if there are only good things to tell?" He says and lifts my chin.

"Listen if you need me to be just your friend, I can do that. Like I said, I'm patient. Or," he pauses.

"Or?" I ask.

"Or you can let me take you on a date and we can figure out what we feel together." He says.

"I'll think about it." I sigh.

I swear my heart literally skips a beat. He's standing close to me, telling me everything I want to hear, but I can't give him anything. He deserves someone who knows who they are and what they want. Someone who can handle the way other girls outwardly eye-fuck him. Someone who is capable of loving him back.

"Friends is all I can handle."

"Got it." He smiles, unaffected and turns to walk facing forward again. "Just let me know if you feel like you can handle more."

He can't be serious. I need to tell him it'll never happen. That he shouldn't wait around for me and should find someone else. So why are the words getting stuck on my tongue? We walk in silence for a few more minutes before I realize that isn't where mine and Skye's conversation ended.

"So what else did you hear?" I ask, not even sure I want to know the answer.

The grin that takes over his face is breathtaking, his dimples deepening in his cheeks. If I didn't know any better, I'd think he just won the lottery.

"I heard Skye say that you're crushing on me. And I also didn't hear you deny it."

Fuck, I was hoping he didn't hear that part. My eyes are open wide in embarrassment and I'm staring at the ground, unable to speak. I look over at him briefly and he's still wearing that beautiful smile.

"So tell me something only your friends know." He says, breaking the silence. I'm grateful for the subject change as I'm not sure my cheeks can possibly be any more red.

"I don't know." I shrug, bumping my arm against his playfully "I feel like I've already told you a lot, meanwhile you've been very tight lipped."

"Hmm... you're right. Ask me anything." He says.

I think for a moment, pondering which one of the thousands of questions that are flooding my mind to go with.

"What's the story behind your tattoo?" I ask, trying to keep things light.

"What?" He asks.

"I saw part of your tattoo this morning, and I was curious what it is." I say.

"Well, I have a few so I guess it depends on which one you're asking about. I've got this one," he says, lifting his jacket and shirt to show a sign on his ribs with the letter B. "It's the sign for 'I love you' for my sister Birdie."

"Birdie and Sunshine?" I giggle.

"Yeah yeah, again mom. Hippie. And then I have a treble clef here," he points to his jacketed elbow to a tattoo I've definitely noticed more than once, "I got that when I decided to major in musical theater. And the last one I can't really show you without undressing in the middle of campus, but it's a clock and gears. It's for my mom." He says, and I swear I see his smile falter slightly for the briefest of moments.

I look at him inquisitively, patiently waiting for him to continue.

"She died from lung cancer three years ago, and I wish I had more time with her."

I stop in my tracks, the feeling of guilt overtaking me. I shouldn't have asked. Of course it had to be meaningful when he said it was for his mom.

"Oh my God, I'm so sorry." I say.

"Hey, no need to feel bad," he says, swinging an arm around my shoulders and urging me forward to continue our walk. "We got more time with her than we thought we would so I was lucky. Didn't mean to bring the mood down. Ask me something else."

"No, no, you didn't. I'm the one that asked. I don't want to be too nosy or like, make you talk about something you don't want to."

"Seriously, it's okay. Ask away," He reassures.

"Hmm... I'm assuming from the tattoo, you're close to your sister?" I ask.

"Very. She's one of my best friends. I think it helped that there's so much time between us. I was twelve when she was born. When we found out she was deaf, I stepped into a protector role pretty quickly. It annoys the shit out of her." He stops and gestures to the building in front of us. "Here we are."

I nod, trying desperately to hide the fact that my stomach is doing backflips.

"Yeah, I guess I'll see you in ASL tomorrow?"

He gives me a quick smile and a nod before he pulls me into a tight hug and heads toward his class.

I watch for a moment as a girl catches up with him and walks next to him before heading to my class. A twinge of jealousy hits me like a ton of bricks. Of course he's popular. Why wouldn't he be?

The first week of juggling class and work is easy considering most classes were just reviewing syllabuses and easing us in. Sunshine walks me to the humanities every time after comp and texts me nearly every day, sending goofy memes or quick check-ins, my heart rate accelerating every time I see his name across my screen.

Skye and Aubrey are sitting on the couch watching reruns of "Friends" when I come into the apartment. Fucking finally it's the weekend.

"Hellooooooo!" Skye turns on the couch to face me and I see Aubrey cuddled up to her.

"Hey Skye, hey Aubrey." I say.

"Hey Mia! We're going to a party tonight. I don't suppose you want to come?" Aubrey asks.

"Yeah! Come on, little hermit. Be social with us." Skye teases.

"I think I'm partied out for a little while. Will you guys be home for dinner? I was going to make some shrimp scampi and noodles."

"Oh no, we'll be gone by then. But, maybe *Sunshine* is free," Skye teases and I roll my eyes.

She's teased me relentlessly all week about him, which really sucks because I'm *dying* to talk to someone about him, but I know if I give away any of my giddiness it'll just make it ten times worse than it is now.

"Sunshine? When did that happen?" Aubrey asks.

"Oh no, it didn't, they're *friends*." Skye laughs.

"Okay, you guys are, like, close to him or something, right?" I ask, my hands on my hips.

"Yeah, we have a little group that hangs out sometimes. It used to be me, Aubrey, Sunshine, and another girl, Giselle, from the theater department but she graduated and moved." She gets a sly smile, "Why do you ask?"

"Just curious," I shrug and plop down on the couch next to Aubrey.

"Sure you are," she giggles, stretching out her words.

"Come on, Skye, don't do that. I barely know him." I bite on my thumb nail.

"Okay, okay..." She holds her hands up in defeat. "I hear you loud and clear. No more Sunshine talk. Can I just say one more thing and then we can squash it forever?"

I gesture for her to continue, annoyed.

"Don't forget that you came here so *you* can be happy. If you think he will make you happy, then you need to go for it. Maybe not now, but I think eventually you're going to need to be open to it. Anyone who has seen you two together can see that there's something there that's more than friendly. You'll have to stop being so stubborn and just give in." Skye says.

"Are you done now?" I ask.

"Yep. Won't bring it up again." She says.

The worst part is what she's saying makes sense and I know she's right.

"Oh, I've got something." Aubrey chimes in. "If it helps, he's a great stage kisser."

I can't help the laugh that comes out at Skye's shocked face as she wraps her whole body around Aubrey's and says "mine."

While they continue their quick marathon of Friends and getting ready for the party during commercials, I start on dinner. I've never been good at cooking for one, so I end up making way more than necessary. Skye and Aubrey emerge from her room, looking like something out of a magazine, as per usual. Aubrey is wearing a short silky green dress that pops against her caramel skin and brings out some green tones in her hazel eyes. Her short bronze hair is its typical kinky-curled style and frames her face. Next to her, Skye is wearing a short yellow dress that hugs her slim body. Her blonde hair lays wavy on her shoulders and she's wearing her typical dark eye makeup. I swear, they could both be supermodels. Skye walks up behind me and pops a piece of shrimp in her mouth, then groans in delight.

"You cooking for an army, Mi?" Aubrey asks.

"Portioning out dry noodles is hard," I laugh, "You sure you guys aren't hungry before you go?"

"No, we're good. But you know who probably is?" Skye raises her eyebrows suggestively, laughing, before they head toward the door. "Don't wait up!"

I plop down on the couch, not quite ready to eat yet, and look out the window. The sky is so gloomy, all dark with sleet falling quickly as I watch Skye and Aubrey hop into their rideshare. The pinging of my phone pulls me from my thoughts, my heart skipping a beat at the possibility of who it might be, but immediately regulating when I see Mom's name.

> You can't ignore me forever, Mia.

Damn it. I may not be able to ignore her forever, but I can definitely continue to ignore her for now. I stare down at the text message for a few moments before backing out of it, my thumb automatically hovering over Sunshine's name. I could text him, ask him to come over for dinner... but would I even be able to handle it if he said no? My leg is bouncing up and down frantically, and I don't realize I'm biting my thumbnail again until I taste blood. I pull my thumb away from my mouth, wincing, and inspect it before putting a bandage over it.

I grab the book I got from the library yesterday and settle into the couch, but I can't seem to make it past the first page. Is he busy today? Would he even want to come over? I pick my phone up again, taking my bottom lip between my teeth as I open my text messages, before putting it back down again. The moment the phone hits the coffee table, it pings with a text from Sunshine.

> I'm going to go ahead and assume you're NOT going to the party with Skye and Aubrey.

I can't hide the goofy smile that takes over my face as I stare at the screen, unsure how to respond. On one hand, I definitely don't want to be at that party. On the other hand, if Sunshine will be there...

> Me and parties? You're joking, right?

> So what are your plans for tonight?

Honestly, nothing. I just made way too much food and I'm about to sit down to read.

Too much food? Say less, I'm on my way.

I can't tell if he's serious or not, so I head to the bathroom to fix my hair for good measure. I throw some makeup on quickly, but only some light powder and mascara. I don't want it to look like I'm trying too hard, but I also don't want to look like a bum. I try pulling my hair back, but end up taking it back down and running my hands through it so it isn't sticking up all over the place. I'm still staring back at myself hopelessly when the door sounds with a knock. I should've realized that when I mentioned food, Sunshine was completely serious about coming over. I rush over to the door and take a deep breath before opening it.

"It's freezing!" He says with a shiver and I move aside for him to come in. "Give me your body heat."

He sets down the case of beer in his hand and drops a backpack to the floor before exaggerating another shiver and hugging me. I wrap my arms around him and breathe him in. A cold drop of water drops onto my shoulder from his hair.

"Hi," he mutters as he pulls away from me.

"Hi." I giggle in response.

Jeez, I'm pathetic. I need to stop fucking giggling like a little girl with a schoolyard crush.

We stare at each other for a moment and I feel a heat rise within me, like my entire body is going to burst into flames at any moment. My heart feels like it's going a mile a minute, and the butterflies have returned to my stomach. I allow myself to stare at his plush lips for a brief moment, wondering what it'd be like to taste him before I shake the thought away.

"Let's eat," I stammer and move back toward the kitchen, grabbing bowls from the cabinet.

"So tell me more," I say, sitting next to him at the table with two heaping bowlfuls of pasta. "I want to learn more about you."

"Ok," he says, "I grew up in Des Moines. It was just me and my mom for a long time and then my stepdad came along followed by my sister. Um... when I started at Eastview I wanted to study English but then that didn't work out so I switched to Sociology... then I hated that so I switched to what I really wanted to do in the first place, which was musical theater."

"Why not just go for that to begin with?" I ask.

"Honestly? I was embarrassed." He laughs. "In hindsight, it's stupid. But I had already dealt with people's comments about a curly-haired guy in the theater all throughout high school, and I didn't didn't want to anymore. Like I said, it was dumb, but it mattered to me at the time."

"Well I think it's awesome. I *love* musicals," I say.

"Which one is your favorite?" He asks.

"Oh hands down, the one you were just in." I laugh.

"Seriously?" He asks, "but it's so sad!"

"Oh yeah, definitely. It's just so *good*, though. Just seeing the different perspectives of why relationships don't work out... the songs... and *your* voice... I don't know how you don't have girls throwing themselves at you left and right."

"Oh I do." He laughs.

"So modesty is one of your strong suits then?" I laugh and he gives me a big grin.

"I'm just not interested in fucking around anymore, you know? If I date someone, it's because I can potentially see a future with them. I'm not about dating for the sake of dating."

Who even is this guy? In all the movies, all you see with college guys is keg stands, booty calls, and one night stands.

"What about you? What's your favorite musical?" I ask, changing the subject before we hit dangerous territory.

"Too many to name. There are so many good ones. I probably have to go Singin' In the Rain. It was the first lead role I landed when I was in 7th grade. It's when my love for musicals really took off. It's also when I realized that I am *not* a natural baritone. I think that's why I liked it though. I really had to work for it."

"That's so awesome. It's a good one for sure." I twirl my pasta around on my fork.

"My turn to ask questions," he says.

"Okay fine, you get three questions," I say.

"Ooh." He rubs his palms together in excitement. "Okay... hmm. When you graduate, do you want to stay in Iowa?"

"I haven't really thought about it." I shrug. " On one hand I want to be close to my brother, but on the other hand I would love to be far from my mother."

He nods, completely focused on me since he finished his food.

"What about the little bit of free time you get? What do you like to do?"

"Oh, that one's easy." I laugh. "I like to read or watch movies."

"Yeah? What kind?" He asks.

"For movies, horror movies. Sometimes a good comedy or rom-com, as long as it's not an action movie. For books, mostly thrillers, but I'll also read a good fantasy or romance every now and again."

He's silent for a moment while he takes in my answer, and I wonder if I said something wrong.

"Hmm... one more question."

"Actually, you're out of questions. You asked what kind of movies and books I like." I laugh lightly.

"Ahh, out of questions on a technicality." He shakes his head and brings both of our empty plates to the dishwasher before grabbing something from his backpack and moving toward the couch. "Oh, I brought this for you. I saw you have statistics with Dr. Wagner, so I brought my old notes. Thought it could be helpful."

He sits close to me, cracking open beers and showing me his notes. I flip through aimlessly, amused by the doodles in the corners of the pages. We opt to watch a comedy special, his thigh touching mine. We haven't said much since dinner, but I like just being around him. Despite the fact that we're literally just sitting around watching tv, he hasn't touched his phone once. Doing nothing with him could very quickly become one of my favorite activities. I rest my hand on the couch near his. Maybe if I won't allow myself to be with him, the least I can do is revel in the small moments. I try to sneak glances down at our hands and over to him, wanting so badly for him to grab mine. I slowly inch my hand closer to his so the outside of our hands are touching, as the front door flies open, causing me to jump up.

"MI!!!" Skye shouts and then laughs.

She stumbles through the door, catching herself on the table in front of her, her keys flying to the floor. Aubrey follows right behind her, laughing as well.

"Oh no." I rush over to her and lead her to her room.

"I missed you," she says as we walk, petting the side of my head.

They're completely wasted so I need to get them to her room and sleep before Skye inevitably pukes. Unsurprisingly, as soon as we walk in the door of her room, she upchucks all over her bed. I hold her hair back and Sunshine comes in with a bucket. I rub her back as she empties the contents of her stomach.

"Jesus Jensen, how much did you drink?" He asks.

"I don't know- a little here, a little there. You're here!" She throws her arms around Sunshine in a hug and then leans back to look at him. "Have you guys kissed yet?"

"Come on, I need to get you to the couch so I can change your sheets."
I sigh and help her up.

Sunshine drapes one of her arms over his shoulder and I take the other.

"I'm serious, Mi. I love you and I just want you to be happy. He's a *good guy*. Like, the *best guy*. I knew you'd love him."

I help Skye lie on the couch and get a cold, wet cloth to place over her forehead. Aubrey has taken a seat at the table near the door, her head buried in her hands as Sunshine squats down in front of her to help her.

I look from Skye to Sunshine before I head toward her room to change her sheets. I check her closet where she keeps them and come up empty. Fuck,

"Okay, come on Boozy, you're sleeping in my room." I help Skye off the couch and Sunshine follows suit, helping Aubrey up.

We help Skye into my room and I tuck her in. Aubrey follows closely behind with Sunshine waiting in the doorway.

"Aww Mia, we don't need to take your bed. We can just sleep on the couch." Aubrey whines, already climbing into bed next to Skye.

"Nah, don't worry about it. There's two of you and only one of me. Sleep well. I'll rinse out the bucket and leave it on the side of the bed."

When I turn back toward the doorway, Sunshine gives me a soft smile and follows me to the couch.

"Do you care if I hang out a little longer? Or did you want me to head out?"

"No, no stay. We should finish this special."

I grab a throw blanket and head back to the couch.

"You cold?" I ask, offering some of the blanket that I've already cuddled up with.

He nods and takes part of the blanket, but it comes up short from where he sits on the couch. He scoots closer to me, his thigh touching mine again.

After a little while, I can feel myself slipping into sleep. I try to fight it, but it's a losing battle.

I wake to a hand stroking my hairline.

"Mia," he whispers.

"Sunshine?" I say, groggily.

"Mia, please don't make me wait anymore." I feel his lips brush my temple. "I want to be with you."

"We can't. I can't." I open my eyes and see him staring down at me.

"You want to though." He says, stroking my hair again.

"I do," I whisper.

"You do what?" He asks.

"I want you," I say, breathless.

"What do you want me to do, baby?" He asks.

"Kiss me." I breathe, closing my eyes.

Just before his lips reach mine, my eyes flutter open and the faint smell of cedarwood and citrus hits me. It's still dark outside but the tv is turned down low with an episode of *Breaking Bad* playing. It takes me a minute to realize I'm laying on Sunshine's shoulder. And not just laying, but fucking drooling. I lift my head slowly, hoping he's asleep too, but feel him shift when I do.

"You okay?" He whispers.

I sit up quickly, wiping at my mouth as I lock gazes with him. He's wearing a look of concern.

"I'm so sorry," I whisper.

That's all I *can* say. How fucking embarrassing. He offers me a warm smile and shakes his head.

"Don't be, it doesn't bother me. You looked comfortable, and I didn't want to wake you."

I check the clock on my phone and it's three a.m. This poor guy has been sitting here for like two hours just waiting for me to wake up.

"You should just sleep here," I offer. "It's too late to drive home. I'll sleep on the floor, and you can take the couch."

I move to stand but he grabs my arm.

"I will sleep on the floor. *You* will sleep on the couch." He smiles down at me before standing and grabbing a pillow and blanket from the linen closet.

I know there's no point in fighting him on it— it's clear I won't win. I turn the tv off and curl up on the couch, turning away from where Sunshine makes a makeshift bed on the floor to hide my embarrassment.

"I'm sorry again," I say in the darkness after many minutes of silence.

"Seriously don't be," he whispers and I can almost *hear* his smile.

"Are you asleep," I whisper to the darkness after several more minutes.

"No, what's up?" He whispers back.

"I can't sleep," I say.

"How come?"

"I usually listen to music until I fall asleep."

He chuckles. "I could sing."

"Wait, would you?"

"It was a joke, but if you really want me to..."

"I mean, your voice is nothing short of amazing. I'd be lying if I said I didn't want to hear it again."

I swear my heart soars as he quietly sings "Blackbird" by The Beatles, as if he went through my sleep playlist and chose the most frequently played song. I'm dying to stay awake to hear the end of the song but I fall asleep quickly.

When I wake again, it's morning. Sunshine is lying cuddled on the floor, though his shirt is now off.

I walk quietly to where he's sleeping, and lay a few feet in front of him, my face parallel to his. I watch as his chest rises and falls in a deep slumber and hope he doesn't wake with my laying here. Why did that have to be a dream? Or, on the other hand, why did I have to wake up? If I wasn't pining over him before, I sure as hell am now. But I can't give in. There's something in my brain shouting "this is a horrible idea!" and I can't just ignore that. I reach out and brush a curl away from his forehead carefully so I don't wake him.

"I swear to God if I ever drink again, just shoot me." Skye says as she walks from my room to the living room. She looks from Sunshine to me and back to Sunshine. I scramble to my feet and move to her quickly.

"Wh-" she starts, but I clap my hand over her mouth before she has a chance to give me away.

We both hear Sunshine groan into a yawn and I can't help but take in the view of his toned muscles flexing. I can feel Skye looking at me but I still can't peel my eyes away.

"Uh...huh. That tracks. Anyways, we need food and ibuprofen, stat." She says, breaking me out of my trance.

"Alright," Sunshine says, throwing his blanket off and standing. I have to force myself to stop staring. "Come on, old lady, let's get you some McDonalds."

Skye smiles graciously and grabs a sweater.

"You want anything?" Sunshine asks.

I swear if I open my mouth to speak at this moment, anything that comes out would be absolute gibberish, so I just shake my head no.

He gives me a tight hug before grabbing his keys off the table near the door and heading out with Skye, leaving Aubrey asleep in my bed.

I fall back onto the couch and let out a frustrated groan, pulling the blankets up and over my face.

Why did I have to have that fucking dream?

5

It's been weeks and I still can't stop thinking about that dream. What does it mean? And why do I feel like I can still feel his lips on my head?

Sunshine has still been hanging around our apartment, but I'm grateful that the overnights have stopped. I don't know how long I'd be able to keep my composure if I kept waking up to his naked torso.

Sunshine takes his usual seat next to me in English Comp before class starts. Every time I see him, I get butterflies and my heart starts to race, as if I *don't* see him nearly every day.

"You okay, Mia?" He whispers as class starts, putting a hand on my arm, and I nod, looking forward.

I thought for sure the more we hung out, the easier it would get to be his friend, but it's only getting harder and harder to be around him. I steal a glance at him during class and he's leaning back in his seat, relaxed but paying attention. When I see a small smile play on his lips, I realize that he's noticed me staring and quickly look forward.

After class, he stands and waits for me as he has every time to walk me to the science center. We walk side by side, both bundled from the freezing weather. Man, I can't wait for Spring to hit.

"You want to hang out this weekend? We can hang at my place for a change and I can make you, Skye, and Aubrey dinner," he asks and I groan.

"That sounds infinitely better than my plans. Unfortunately I'm going to visit the devil this weekend for the first time since I've been back. And by devil I mean my mother."

"Ouch." He laughs. "That sucks. Oh well, another time then. When do you leave?"

"After classes today. I'm supposed to stay there all weekend. Evidently my mom wants to 'smooth things over,'" I say, using air quotes. "Basically it's going to be a shitshow."

The walk to the science center feels shorter every time we walk it as I crave more and more one on one time with Sunshine.

"You'll have to let me know how the shitshow goes then," he wraps me into a hug and I try to savor the scent of him that I won't have all weekend.

I really hope his hoodie still smells like him after the third or fourth wash... I need to make myself give it back.

I watch as he walks away and the familiar red-head catches up, walking alongside him. The pang of jealousy is completely unwelcome and unnecessary. It's not like he's mine.

Hopefully, the inevitable chaos of this weekend will keep me distracted from this infatuation with Sunshine.

I exhale a long, shaky breath as I pull up to my childhood home. I look up at the house and through the window of my bedroom. If I stare at it long enough, will I have to go inside or will it just disappear?

"Mia!!" I hear Frankie yell as he runs out of the house and toward my car.

I smile and hop out of the driver's seat, throwing my arms around him in a hug. Not too long ago I was able to pick him up and spin him around, but now he's almost my height and will probably pass me up soon. It's been far too long since I've seen him and I don't think I realized just how much I missed him until he came running out, erasing all of my anxiety.

"Hey kid! How are you? How's school?"

"School sucks. Mom keeps telling me that I need to get better grades and that you *always* got good grades," Frankie sighs.

"Yeah well, don't listen to her. Are you trying your best?" I ask.

"Of course I am."

"That's all that matters." I fluff his hair and he playfully slaps my hand away.

When we make our way inside, my arm slung around his shoulders, I notice Mom sitting at the kitchen table with a coffee mug and a book in hand. I swear, my love for reading is probably the only thing I inherited from her.

"Mia," she says.

"Mom," I acknowledge with a nod and head for my room, not quite ready to face her just yet.

My phone buzzes in my pocket and I smile as I check the incoming text.

> **Did you make it ok?**

> I did, thanks. I have to study for this Ed exam so I think I'm going to shut my phone off.

> **Roger dodger. Happy studying. I'll miss you this weekend!**

He'll miss me. Five words and I'm giddy all over again. I am so royally fucked. After powering my phone down, I start studying my flash cards, but it's not the same. I miss Sunshine's corny jokes and goofy acronyms that help me remember the material. He's made studying actually kind of fun over the last two months.

"Frankie! Come help me study!" I yell, hoping his company may help me remember some of this stuff.

After Frankie rushes to my room and jumps on my bed, I read aloud to try to help myself remember. He watches as I continue to read aloud and falls asleep in my bed. It's a struggle, but I manage to carry him to his room and tuck him, pulling the blankets up over his shoulders.

"Mia," Mom calls from the kitchen as I head back to my own room.

"Yeah?" I call out.

"Come here. Let's talk."

And so the battle begins. I take a deep breath and head toward the kitchen. Mom is sitting at the kitchen table, sipping from her favorite mug adorned with the phrase "please cancel my subscription to your excuses," and wearing a nightgown. Her blonde hair is pinned up in curlers and she glances my way, waving to the open seat across from her.

"I made some lavender tea if you'd like some." She offers, motioning to the tea kettle on the stove.

I've never been a tea drinker. It tastes like hot, dirty water. I've told her this several times, yet every time she makes it, she offers me a cup and gets annoyed when I decline.

"I'm okay, thank you."

We sit in silence for several moments while she looks me over. The fire behind her disapproving eyes makes me hope that she'll give up on this conversation before it starts. When she got word that I left Duke, I knew she'd be pissed. She had already been nagging me to "make things right with James" but I'm sure my leaving was the nail in her coffin. Of course, I knew she was going to find out after I ran into James while Skye packed my car full of my stuff. I'm sure he was on the phone with his mom before we even pulled out of the parking lot.

"Ok, so I just want to understand." Mom says, finally, pressing her fingers into her temples and closing her eyes.

"Understand what?" I ask.

"You. What happened, Mia? We had a *plan*." She sighs.

"I know we did, Mom, but it didn't feel right. It felt more like your plan than mine."

"No no no, don't turn this around on me. We talked about it. And poor *James*. You know, his parents are crushed too. I had to run interference for you with them while you were off doing who knows what for the past few months. Now luckily they're willing to look past it and James said-"

"Wait, you talked to *James*?" I ask, confused.

"Well yes, of course. You may be okay with ruining your life but I won't let you. James loves you. Now, he won't transfer here, so you'll have to transfer back. I spoke to your advisor and I had to pull *a lot* of strings but they said-"

My mind is spinning and I can't help the small, incredulous laugh that escapes me.

"Stop!" I exclaim. "Please just stop! *This* is what I want. I don't *want* James. I don't *want* to be a doctor. I don't *want* to go to Duke!"

"Yes well, in about ten years when all you *want* is stability, you will thank me," she responds calmly.

I blink in quick succession to keep the tears from falling down my face. I've never spoken to my mother like that. Never once have I questioned her or stood up for myself, and now I know that even if I had, it wouldn't have mattered. I stare at her, and she stares back wearing a smug, victorious smile.

"So," she says, straightening herself. "I will send some movers to your place with Skye on Monday and you need to contact-"

I cut her off by holding a hand up, signaling for her to stop talking. She's looking at me with her mouth agape, as if this was the single rudest thing I could have done. To be fair, I surprised myself with that one. I can't believe she really thinks that it's all decided. That I'll just comply. She doesn't care what I want or what I need and I don't know that she ever will. The thought alone is enough to bring me to tears again. I can't go back to that place, both literally and emotionally. I can't let this woman, who has no *idea* what's best for me, run my life anymore. I take a deep breath as I stare back at my mother.

"I can't do this." I stand up and walk to Frankie's room.

"See you later little man." I kiss his forehead as he sleeps and head back to my room to pack my clothes.

"Mia, what are you doing?" Mom asks, following me. "You're supposed to stay the weekend."

"I have a test on Monday that I need to be prepared for."

"Right. For your *education* degree," she says, disgusted.

"Bye Mom." I sigh, dejected. "Hopefully someday you can understand that I'm just doing what makes me happy."

On the walk to my car, I power my phone on and shoot a quick text over to Skye.

> I'm headed back

It's pitch black outside and the car's radio reads 11:30PM. It's a thirty minute drive back to Eastview and a small part of me is wishing I waited until morning to leave.

> That bad?!

> Worse, if it's possible.

I set the music up on my phone and start the drive back to the apartment.

Why does she think that she can control my life? And why would she want to? Can't she see how unhappy I was and shouldn't she *want* me to be happy? Isn't that, like, the whole point of parenting? Wanting your kids to live a happy and fulfilled life? The worst part is, I know I can't place all of the blame on her. I've allowed her to control *everything* since I was little. Shit, probably since I was born. Not once did I speak up and say "hey mom I don't think I *want* to be a doctor because blood kind of freaks me out" or "mom I hate student council and I don't want to be on it" or even something as simple as "mom I *hate* when you put my hair in pigtails and I wish you wouldn't." I always did whatever she wanted, no matter what, because I hated seeing her disappointed in me.

My phone rings through my car speakers after about ten minutes and it's Sunshine.

"Hello," I say, trying not to start crying.

"Skye called me. Are you okay?" He asks, his voice filled with a sleepiness that indicates he was probably sleeping.

"No," I choke.

"What happened? Talk to me."

His voice is soft and encouraging so I recount my short visit, allowing a few tears to fall periodically.

"I'll be at your place when you get home," he says.

"No it's okay. You don't have to, it's so late," I say.

"I'll be there when you get home," he repeats, "because I want to."

"Okay," I whisper, still trying not to cry. "I'll see you there."

When I pull into the parking lot, I see Sunshine sitting on the curb outside our apartment wearing his jacket and beanie. I take a deep breath before getting out of my car and heading for the building. He stands when I approach and holds his arms out for me. When he wraps his arms around me into a tight hug, I can't hold it in anymore and I start crying. Not just crying, but full on sobbing, and he just holds me. He strokes my hair with one hand and rubs the length of my back with his other. I feel him kiss the top of my head and something about all of it just feels so *right*. I listen to his heartbeat and try to slow my breathing to match his. When I've calmed a bit, he holds me out at arms length and looks into my eyes.

"Are you okay?" He asks and I shrug. "Who does that? Who calls their kid's ex and begs them to take them back? I'm so sorry."

"It's fine," I say, wiping my tears. "It's fine. I knew it was going to be bad, I just didn't think it would be that bad."

"Well Skye said she's making your favorite midnight snack," he says and gestures toward the door. "Shall we?"

I stare at him a moment before wrapping my arms around his waist again. He wraps his arms around me and holds me a bit longer before putting an arm around my waist while we walk inside.

The scent of freshly baked chocolate chip cookies hits me as soon as we walk in the door and I take a deep inhale.

"Hey baby girl," Skye says, rounding the counter and pulling me into a hug. "I've got your fave in the oven and some sappy rom coms cued up."

"Sounds perfect." I hug her back. "Are you going to stay too?" I turn to look up at Sunshine.

"Nah, I think you need some girl time. I just wanted to be here when you got home."

"Do you want to come over tomorrow?" I ask.

Fuck, I sound desperate.

"Yeah I can probably swing that." He smiles at me.

A coolness hits my cheek as he hugs me goodbye, and I feel a flush of embarrassment. I pull away from his embrace to confirm that he has a rather large wet spot on his jacket from where I'd cried.

"Sorry," I whisper.

"Don't be," he smiles. "I don't mind."

Sunshine offers one more hug as Skye cues up the movie. I lay my head in Skye's lap and she strokes my hair as we watch the movie in silence.

"Do you want to talk about it?" Skye asks as a commercial comes on, talking about some medication with an endless list of side effects.

"No," I shake my head. "I'd rather talk about *anything* else. How are things with you and Aubrey?"

"She's the best," she sighs, lovingly. "She's seen all of my crazy and still loves me, so I feel like that's a major win... we're actually talking about me moving into her apartment after graduation..."

"That's awesome!" I exclaim.

"Are you sure? What will you do?" She asks.

"I don't know," I respond, waving her off without worry. "I'll move into the dorms or something. Don't worry about me. I'm so happy for you!"

I hug her waist, too tired to move and fully hug her.

"You know, you could be happy for *you* too if you'd just give in," she taunts.

"We're just friends." I yawn.

"Come on, anyone who's been in a room with the two of you for more than two seconds knows *that* isn't true. You guys had no hope of being just friends from the moment you met."

"I almost wish he'd never talked to me at the cast party... it would've made things simpler."

"Sunshine hung around the apartment *before* you moved in. You would've met him regardless. It's fate," she teases and I roll my eyes.

We focus on the movie that's returned to the screen and I think about what she said. Fate isn't real; it only exists in stories. If I had met him in different circumstances, would I even feel this way? He appears in my dream and almost kisses me again, leaving me disappointed when I wake up.

6

I'm removing the last of the grilled cheeses I made for lunch from the frying pan when I hear a knock on the door. I smile and rush over to the door, fixing my hair in the mirror before I open it.

"Hey Sunsh-"

I'm cut off by the sight of James standing in my doorway, smiling, and stare with wide eyes.

"Mimi!" He exclaims and pulls me into a tight hug.

"James? Um, what are you doing here?" I ask, shock overwhelming my senses with my arms limp at my sides while he hugs me.

"Well I was going to meet you at your mom's house, but she told me you left early so she gave me your address and I came straight here instead. Aren't you going to invite me in?"

"Um, yeah sure. Come on in." I begrudgingly say and move to the side to allow him inside.

He looks me up and down, probably taking in the various ways my body has changed since we broke up. I thought for sure that I'd feel relieved when I inevitably saw him again, hoping we could pick our friendship back up, but all I feel is the desperate urge for him to leave. He's not tall by any means, standing at five foot seven, but he still feels like he towers over me at five foot two. His sandy blonde hair is slicked back as it usually is and he's wearing his typical dark peacoat that matches his eyes and dark slacks.

Skye walks out of her room but is just as stunned to see James. "James. What the hell are you doing here?"

"Skye," he says, tipping his head in greeting with a smile. "Pleasure as always. I'm here to talk with Mimi."

"Did *Mia* know you were coming?" she asks.

"No, just a happy surprise, right Mimi?" he asks.

"No, not really." Skye responds, arching one of her eyebrows and crossing her arms.

The tension in the air is so thick it's almost hard to breathe.

"It's fine Skye, really." I reassure her and there's another knock at the door. Oh fuck.

James turns and opens the door like he owns the place before I even have a chance to make a move toward it.

"Uh, hi. Are Mia and Skye here...?" Sunshine asks, sounding rightfully confused.

"They are... who are you?" James asks.

I walk over and open the door more so Sunshine can come in.

"James, it's fine. This is my friend Sunshine."

"James? Like James, James?" Sunshine asks quietly, as he pulls me in a quick hug and I nod subtly. He holds out a beautiful bouquet of multicolored tulips. "I thought you guys could liven up the place."

"Thanks." I blush, taking the flowers and heading to the kitchen to find a vase to put them in.

"Ah, a new friend. Pleasure to meet you." James gives Sunshine a firm pat on the back before making his way to me and lowering his voice. "So Mimi you know how I feel about you hanging out with other guys. *Especially* ones bringing you flowers...right?"

As I snip the bottoms of the flowers over the sink, James wraps his arm around my waist and I feel like I'm going to be sick. I step out of his grasp and move to fill the vase with water.

"We're not together anymore, James."

"Yeah that's why I'm here... It's okay, baby, what happened is in the past and we can move on. I forgive you. I can help you start packing and you can move back into our place by next wee-"

He's cut off when Sunshine lets out a half-laugh, half-scoff under his breath, standing by the kitchen counter.

"Uh, is there a problem?" James asks him, confusion evident on his face.

I step between the two of them and face James before it gets ugly.

"Look, I'm so sorry you came all this way. I don't know what my mom said to you but... I'm happy here and I meant what I said when we broke up. I-" I clear my throat. "I don't want to get back together."

James stares at me for a moment, shock evident on his face for a mere moment before he composes himself and straightens. He looks Sunshine over behind me before smiling at me.

"Well, I guess I should have called first. Would you mind if I hung out here for a bit? My plane doesn't leave until late tonight and I'd still love to catch up."

"Um, yeah sure, that would be fine." I shrug.

What else was I supposed to say? No James, please get the fuck out because you're making me really uncomfortable? It's not like he's a bad guy— we just didn't work out.

We all head to the table for lunch and sit in an awkward silence. James is looking me over, scraping his eyes over every inch of my body until I suddenly have no appetite.

"Aubrey's audition is tomorrow, when is yours Parker?" Skye asks, breaking the silence.

"Tuesday," he responds.

"You nervous?" she asks.

"Always." He laughs. "Actually, I was hoping to run my audition by you for some feedback, Mia."

"Yeah." I nod, and it's all I can make myself say.

"Audition for what?" James asks.

"*Heathers*. It's the Spring musical," Sunshine explains.

"Oh," James laughs and then stops when he looks around the table and notices no one else is. "Oh shit, you're serious."

"You good Mi? You've hardly touched your food," Skye asks, changing the subject.

"Uh oh, did someone get a little too snacky before lunch again?" James laughs and I notice Sunshine shift uncomfortably.

I smile sheepishly and stare down at my food.

"How did your bio exam go on Friday?" Sunshine turns his attention toward me.

"I think it was okay but I probably should have studied a little bit more. I'm pretty sure I still passed." I smile at him.

"You wait until the last minute and cram again?" James teases. "I heard you were struggling pretty hard at Duke before you dropped out. Probably not the best time to be slacking."

Sunshine looks between James and me, confusion evident in his face.

"I'm sorry, are we talking about the same Mia?" he asks, "She's one of the hardest working people I've ever met."

"Well, I don't know how long *you've* known her but I've known her since we were like... twelve? Trust me, she talks a good game. I'm pretty sure I even caught her cheating off of me a time or two in high school." James taunts in a teasing tone with a charming smile on his face.

The way he says it is so matter-of-fact that even I almost believe it, even though I have never cheated on anything in my life. Sunshine looks at me confused and I shrug, shaking my head to tell him to leave it alone. James leaves his empty plate at the table and moves to the couch, turning the TV on and flipping it to a sports channel.

"Uh, James. We actually had some movies lined up for today," Skye says from the table.

"Oh come on, Sunshine here doesn't want to watch any of your chick flicks." He looks toward Sunshine. "There's nothing like bonding over baseball, am I right?"

"I'm not huge on sports," Sunshine says with a shake of his head. "Also, this is their apartment. They can watch what they want."

"Yeah, okay, you're right," James says with a smile and stands. "Let's do something. Maybe a game or something? How about some truth or dare?"

He lifts an eyebrow at me in challenge and I look at the ground.

"Oh, so you *do* remember, Mimi. You guys will love this story. Okay so we were at Chris Ube's house and our friend Luna dared Mimi to take a shot of whiskey and she did, and then boom! Projectile vomit all over the floor." He laughs. "It was so gross."

Sunshine and Skye are mirroring each other at the table with crossed arms and a look of revolt. Great. From the look on his face, any chance of Sunshine being interested in me just went out the window from a stupid story about how I couldn't hold my alcohol at fourteen.

"Dude, what's your problem?" Sunshine asks, to my surprise.

"What do you mean? No problem over here." James shrugs. "Just reminiscing on old times."

"You're being an asshole James," Skye says "Like, more than usual."

I watch as James takes in his surroundings. Both Skye and Sunshine look equally pissed off, and despite the fact that this seems like it's going to go very badly, very quickly, I can't make myself say anything. James's eyes darken and his smile turns almost sarcastic.

"Am I? I mean, I *did* get dumped on my ass," he gestures to me. "Pretty brutally too I might add. Did you tell them what you said to me?"

I'm frozen to the spot, still unable to say anything. It's all I can do to stare at the ground and will my tears not fall. I will not cry in front of him again.

The knots in my stomach grow and I feel like I'm going to puke. Sunshine puts his hand on my arm comfortingly, his attention focused on me rather than James.

"I'm just not *it* for her," he says to the room. "That's what she said. So you guys think *I'm* the asshole? Who the fuck does that? She said she'd *marry* me and then she just up and left out of nowhere. And then her mom calls and says 'oh you know she knows she made a huge mistake and you're the best thing that's ever happened to her and she can't live without you.' So I figure I love her, I need to give her another shot."

He stands and moves closer to me, staring me down with more anger and hatred than I've ever seen from him.

"So what, Mia? You just wanted to reject me twice? Well I'm not fucking begging. God, what was I thinking coming here for *you?* You're nothing but a worthless, stuck-up prude."

He's standing over me, staring me down and speaking in that deadly calm voice that always sent chills down my spine as I stare at the ground, wishing I was anywhere but here. His words cut deep and I am swallowed by guilt when Sunshine's chair pushes back quickly and he steps in between us.

"You need to go." Sunshine says.

"Dude for real? Did you hear anything I just said? *Clearly,* you don't know her very well. Don't fall for it. She's *manipulating* you. Sure she's probably making you feel great right now. Talking you up, giving you those flirty gazes, and making you think she actually gives a shit... until she just up and leaves. We had everything set- the wedding venue, the DJ, the caterer... and my parents were paying for *all* of it. She would have been set *for life,* but she just walked away like it was nothing. Like *I* was nothing. You can't fix her man, she's too far gone," he tells Sunshine and then looks past him at me, "And I was so fucking *nice* to you. You think you're ever going to find someone who's as *patient* with you as I was?"

"Seriously James, get the hell out of our apartment. If anyone in this room is a manipulative asshole, it's you," Skye chimes in.

Before James can respond, Sunshine grabs his arm and leads him to the door.

"You've clearly overstayed your welcome, if you had any in the first place, and you need to leave before one of these fine ladies calls the cops," Sunshine says and dangles James' backpack by the handle.

"Oh fuck you man," James snatches his backpack and turns back to me, pointing his finger at me. "And fuck you Mia. Honestly, I feel bad for you. You think you're so much better than me, but I'm so far out of your league it's not even funny. You're going to spend your entire life alone and miserable."

Sunshine is ushering him out the door as he speaks and slams the door once he's fully outside. I don't think I've ever seen Sunshine angry, but he's wearing a scowl so deep as Skye scoffs and rolls her eyes at the door. I put my face in my hands and cry silently. Skye and Sunshine are on either side of me at the table as I cry and Sunshine rubs my back in slow circles.

"Damn it, look at me, Mia. You are not any of the horrible things that *asshole* has ever called you. You are beautiful and smart and funny and kind and one of the most hardworking people I've ever met. Do *not* let him do this to you again, Mi. You've come too far," Skye strokes the hair on the side of my head as I lean into Sunshine's touch.

I nod slowly, but I can't keep from crying and Sunshine pulls me into his chest. He lets me cry as he runs his fingers through my hair.

"See, this is what I meant by I'm a mess." I cry into his chest.

He pulls me back and looks in my eyes, rubbing the tears away from my cheekbones with his thumbs.

"You're not a mess. That guy is a dick."

He continues to caress my cheek and I have to remind myself to breathe. When the tears and my breathing have slowed, his face breaks out in a wide, mischievous smile.

"I have an idea," he says.

I look at him curiously.

"Skye, we haven't been to Snowy Owl yet this year." He turns to Skye and her face lights up in the same mischievous smile.

"Oh I don't know that Mia's ready for Snowy Owl." She responds in a challenging tone.

"What's Snowy Owl?" I ask with a sniffle.

"You'll see." Sunshine smiles at me. "Go get changed. Wear something warm. I'm going to swing by my place really quickly and I'll pick you up. We'll grab Aubrey on the way out too."

I give him a slight smile, wipe the last of the tears from my eyes, and take Skye's hand to get up.

Normally anything that involves wearing something warm is an automatic absolutely not for me, but I'm kind of excited as I ponder over what Snowy Owl could be. Maybe an outdoor restaurant? One of those igloo bars? Even better, an ice cream place? Just how warm am I supposed to dress? It's snowing outside, but will we even be outside?

I opt for leggings underneath a pair of jeans with a long sleeved shirt and a hoodie. Better to have layers to take off.

Skye looks me over when I walk out of the room.

"You're going to want a heavy jacket... and gloves.... And a hat."

"Where the heck are we going?" I ask.

"You'll see," she replies with a smile, her voice rising and falling in a sing-song rhythm.

Sunshine puts the car in park near a big open field surrounded by woods. There are no buildings anywhere in sight, so I am left utterly confused.

"Is this the part where you guys kill me and bury my body in the woods?" I laugh, as I close my car door behind me.

"Oh shut up, you can't get rid of us that easily." Skye waves me off.

Skye links her arms in mine and brings me into the open field and I see a large decline leading into the woods.

A hill. We're on a big ass, snowy hill.

Sunshine and Aubrey walk up behind us with several plastic sleds in tow.

"This," Sunshine says as throws his arms out, "is Snowy Owl. We come sledding here every year, and this year you get to join that tradition."

"Sledding?" I ask, disgusted. Skye nods excitedly, putting one of the sleds on the ground. "I hate sledding."

"Really?" Sunshine looks at me in surprise.

"Well, it's not so much that I hate it as I've avoided doing it because I'm pretty sure I *will* hate it."

"Yeah, but you also haven't gone sledding with us." Skye laughs and takes a seat in her sled, Aubrey sliding in behind her.

I chew on the inside of my cheek as Sunshine sets a sled beside me, and Skye and Aubrey take off on their sled, whooping and hollering as they gain speed.

"Do you want me to go with you?" He asks, rubbing my cheek with his thumb until I stop biting it.

For once, I couldn't be more grateful for the cold, since it can be blamed for the redness I'm sure his touch is causing on my cheeks. I nod and take the front seat on the sled. When he slides in behind me, straddling his legs on either side of me, I can feel the heat of his body against mine.

"I'll steer us, you just sit back and enjoy," Sunshine murmurs in my ear.

Sunshine pushes the sled forward with his feet until we're flying down the steep hill quickly. With the smile that overtakes my face, I'm sure any outsider would never guess my ex fiancé just tore me to shreds a mere hour ago. The wind is freezing as the snow comes down around us, but I am loving the feeling of freedom as we fly down the hill and level out at the bottom.

Sunshine leans forward to look at me with a smile.

"Oh man, you really *did* hate it. It looks like you had the worst time ever." He teases before he calls out to Skye and Aubrey, who likely can't hear him a the top of the hill. "Guys! She hates it! We need to pack up!"

I giggle in response.

"Again?" He asks and I nod excitedly.

I follow him back up the hill on the side, with him dragging the sled behind him. I did *not* wear the right shoes for this as the snow seeps through, freezing my feet. The hill is a hard climb and Sunshine loops his arm around mine to help.

"Do you want to try by yourself?" he asks when we reach the top.

"Hell no." I laugh. "I don't trust myself to steer it."

Realistically, I could probably figure out how to steer it, but damn if I don't want to feel his body against mine again.

I hop in the front of the sled again and Sunshine takes his spot behind me. As we fly down the hill, the air feels colder than before. It's hard to see between the snow coming down and the wind making me squint, but I can just barely make out a tree that we are headed right for. Sunshine puts his foot down to try to steer us away from it, but the sled isn't budging, as if it's determined to crash. I take a deep breath and brace myself for impact when I feel Sunshine wrap his arms around my body and throw us both to the side as the sled makes contact with the tree.

"Mia? Are you okay?" He panics, and hovers over me.

The only thing I can do is laugh. Harder than I've laughed in a while. I almost miss the shift in his face from concern to relief as he hovers over me and lets out a small laugh of his own.

"Did you get hurt at all?" He asks, his face inches from mine.

It takes everything in me to focus on my reply instead of his plush lips as he waits for my answer. I shake my head slowly and hear footsteps in the snow as Sunshine quickly sits up, the loss of his body heat disappointing.

"Let's go back to the apartment," Skye says. "My toes are freezing. We'll watch all of the corny rom coms we had set up for today and remind you that there are good guys in the world."

There has to be good guys out there somewhere, right? Or even here? Sitting in the snow next to me? Trying to get me to give him the time of day and I keep pushing him off? I just know I couldn't handle when he would eventually hate me, too.

Skye sits first when we arrive back at the apartment and Aubrey takes the seat next to her, cuddling up, while Sunshine and I take the other end of the couch, leaving me sandwiched between Sunshine and Skye. Between sledding and the emotional toll of this morning, I barely make it halfway through the first movie before my head relaxes against the back of the couch and I close my eyes, somewhere in between asleep and awake.

"Is she asleep?" I hear Sunshine ask in a hushed tone, before continuing, "So that guy is a real piece of work, huh?"

"Ugh, he's the *worst*." Skye groans. "I've literally hated him since the moment I met him. Mi's parents and his parents are like, super tight though. It's why our moms aren't friends anymore, but there wasn't shit they could do to keep me away from her."

"She's lucky to have you," Sunshine says.

"She'll always have me whether she likes it or not," Skye says, and I feel her move a piece of hair behind my ear.

"What the fuck is his deal anyways?" Aubrey asks.

There's a moment of silence before Skye speaks up again.

"He's just an asshole, but like a subtle asshole. Like, you know how some people give these backhanded compliments or make rude comments but then laugh it off, so you're not sure if they're joking or not? That's him.

I don't know for sure, but I think he fucked with her head a bit. Like, we'd be on the phone, right? And then out of nowhere, I'd hear him in the background complaining that they don't spend enough time together and she's on the phone too much, blah blah blah, and suddenly she'd have to go. They *lived* together. They had all the same classes. He saw her *all the time*. He just wanted to be her whole world. He didn't want her to have friends that weren't his friends. She was literally going to classes, working out, and spending time with him. That was it... There are so many times when he'd be gone and she would call me *sobbing* because of something he said or did, and I'd tell her what an asshole he was, and she'd just make excuses for him. 'Oh he's just having a bad day' or 'Oh he didn't mean it like that, I'm just being too sensitive'... She didn't talk to anyone but him. She didn't see anyone but him. It was like she was afraid of upsetting him and I never really understood *why*. I mean, I know she's all about pleasing her mom but there has to be more to it. I don't know, their relationship is so damn confusing to me. For the entire five years they were together, I felt like I had lost my best friend because it was like she turned into a different person... And the more time I spent with them together, the more I couldn't even be *mad* at *her*. He was so... crafty. Even charming sometimes. He could twist any situation to make things her fault. And her mom... God, don't even get me started on fucking Patty. She was so interested in the fact that his family had money and that she could bullshit around with her friends that she would make excuses for him too! She'd tell Mia 'don't be so sensitive' or 'well he's a man and you need to take care of him.' It's all so fucked..." Skye lets out a long breath. "Sorry, I will never not fucking hate that man."

Ouch. I can't pretend that didn't suck to hear. Surely it wasn't all that bad... We had our good moments too... right? Why *did* I stay? Several moments have passed and both Sunshine and Aubrey have stayed silent aside from a deep sigh that Sunshine released immediately after.

"I know I may be a biased, but she deserves to be treated like a fucking queen, Parker," Skye sighs. "She's one of the best humans on this planet, and so are you. She needs someone like you to take care of her and dote on her and remind her that she is an amazing fucking person and deserves the world... You like her, don't you?"

"I do, very much so, but I'm trying to just be here for her in a way that is comfortable to her... I don't want to push her into anything," Sunshine says.

"Then ask her out!" Skye whisper-yells.

"I'm not going to do something she isn't ready for. She knows I'm interested. I won't push her, Skye."

Boy if that doesn't make my stomach flip upside down. He's still interested. It's been months and he's *still* interested. I'm desperate to hear the rest of their conversation, but sleep inevitably wins.

When I wake up in my bed, Sunshine is sleeping next to me, cuddled up behind me. *What the fuck?* I turn to face him and he's lying awake.

"Good morning, beautiful." He smiles and kisses my forehead, still holding me.

"What are you doing here?" I ask.

"Do you want me to go?" He asks and I look at him confused before ultimately shaking my head "no."

I don't want him to go. Everything about this feels right. Like I'm finally feeling a sense of weightlessness. He pulls me close to him and runs a hand in my hair at the side of my head.

"Stop fighting this," he whispers, his face inches from mine.

"I don't want to fight it anymore," I whisper and he closes his eyes, moving his face closer to mine.

I sit up with a startle as my alarm blares next to me. I'm practically panting. Another fucking dream. I turn my alarm off and fall back on my bed.

Fuck.

When I leave my bedroom, I half expect to find Sunshine on the couch, but he's not there. I check on Skye, and she and Aubrey are cuddled up in her bed, fast asleep.

With dreams like that, I don't know how much longer I'm going to be able to fight this.

7

I walk out of the library and feel almost instantly grateful that winter is over when the light spring breeze hits my bare arms. Most people have already left campus for Spring Break so I expected to have an easy shift, but the library was almost eerily empty. During the walk to my car in the adjacent lot, I take in the scenery and inhale the slight floral scent of all the flowering trees. The campus is so much more beautiful when there's more life to it.

I'm dreading going back to the apartment. With Skye and Aubrey in Cabo, it just feels so lonely there. What the hell am I going to do when she graduates in a few months? I suppose I could always move back in with my mom and commute from there... though I haven't exactly forgiven her for springing James on me a few months ago... nor have I even talked to her in months despite her plethora of calls. Either the dorms or a one bedroom it is, I guess. Not that I can really afford either option without taking out even more loans.

As I drive toward the apartment, I come to the light for Sunshine's street. He didn't leave town for Spring Break, so he's probably home, and I don't think he'd care if I popped in... I make a right, and head towards his house. When I arrive, Sunshine is mowing the lawn so I decide to sit in my car for a few moments and take in the sight of him. He's wearing a tight sleeveless shirt that he pulls up from the bottom to wipe sweat off of his face, and I can't help but stare at his abs as he does. Between constantly hanging out and the dreams that he's been the star of for months, to say I'm having a difficult time would be a huge understatement. He stops the lawn mower when he notices my car and offers me a wave. I take a breath after turning off my car and head toward him.

"Hey Mia!" He smiles at me, his dimples popping out instantly. "This is a nice surprise."

I smile back at him and wrap my arms around his waist, hugging him, and resting my head on his chest. Breathing him in, I expect him to smell, but he doesn't. How the hell doesn't he smell?

"I'm a bit sweaty." He laughs, but wraps his arm around me.

"I don't care," I say against his chest, closing my eyes and soaking in the physical contact.

Between shifts at the library and the diner, I've barely seen Sunshine during the break and I almost forgot how much I missed him.

"You okay?" He murmurs, and I realize that I've been hugging him for just a fraction too long.

"Sorry." I blush and pull away from him. "I just missed you, I guess."

"I missed you, too. Why don't you head inside? I've just got a little bit left and then I'll join you."

When I head through the front door, I inhale the smell of spring. There's a draft in the house with all of the windows open, so I grab my favorite blanket off of the blanket ladder in the corner before sitting in the bay window with the new Krista Sayer book I picked up on the way home yesterday. I open the hardcover and inhale the scent of the new pages, ready to delve into a new thriller universe, but I get distracted when Sunshine appears before the window in the corner of my eye. He's stripped his shirt off as he squats, gathering weeds from the edge of the garden bed. I try to focus on the book, but I can't help but sneak glances at him. When he walks back inside, I force my eyes back to the pages. Fuck, I haven't even made it past the first page.

"I'm going to hop in the shower and then we can hang out? Want to grab dinner or something?" He asks, grabbing a pillow off the nearby couch and handing it to me. I place it behind my back and cuddle into the spot.

"Oh, sure. That would be great." I look up from my book at his bare chest.

Despite the fact that I looked back down as quickly as I looked up, I can still see the cocky smile he wears from the corner of my eye.

"Slow start?" He asks, gesturing to my book.

"Uh, yep," I say, not looking up.

I hear him let out a small laugh before hearing his footsteps up the stairs towards his room. I let out a breath that I'd been holding because holy fuck, I'd almost forgotten how good he looks without a shirt. And how much he *knows* it.

I'm fully engrossed in the world of *A Perfect Lie* when Sunshine reemerges at the bottom of the stairs, shirtless yet again. His curls are wet and he's wiping at them with a towel, trying to shake the remainder of the water off.

"Good book?" He asks.

"Great book," I reply. "Do we need to take you to the store or something? Or do you have some kind of fabric allergy?"

He gives me a confused, playful look.

"Well clearly you're lacking shirts." I tease, gesturing to his bare torso.

"You mean this?" He holds a shirt up in his other hand and throws it over his shoulder.

"Yeah, that. Can you put it on please?" I laugh.

"Why Mia? Don't like what you see?" He asks, laughing and putting his shirt on.

I place my bookmark on the corner of the page and close the book, looking up at him.

"You know that's not fair," I murmur as he sits next to me on the window seat.

"Not fair? What's not fair is watching you try to subtly brush away goosebumps every time I touch you." He places a hand on my arm and sure enough they are there. "What's not fair is the way you blush every time I say something even remotely nice to you. What's not fair is the way you wrap your arms around me when we hug— like you don't want to be anywhere else. But you know what's really not fair? Watching you self-sabotage. Unless my signals are crossed, what's not fair is you keeping yourself from something that could be great."

My heart nearly melts at his sincerity and a wave of guilt hits me.

"Sunshine..." I start.

"We don't have to talk about it. We're friends, right?" He offers a small smile, and gently pats my leg before standing. "No stress, Mia."

I set my book on the window seat and fold the blanket I'd been using while Sunshine moves to the couch, turning the television on. I can't help but feel kind of sad. A large majority of me knows that he's right. I've had a huge crush on him for months and it's pretty clear at this point that it's not going away. On the other hand, a smaller but just as significant part of me can't let go of the fact that Sunshine has quickly become one of my best friends. Given everything that's happened, I can't afford to lose that. Not again. I feel tears prick my eyes as I allow myself a moment to imagine what it would be like to be his. The always-fresh flowers that would sit on my counter, the endless string of compliments that would be thrown my way, the way he'd do everything in his power to make things as easy as possible for me... He's too good and I'm too damaged. Too insecure, too clingy, too jealous, and just plain too much. I'm not capable of love, so I don't want him to waste any more his time. He deserves better. He deserves to be happy.

The TV brightens with the title screen of some video game and Sunshine settles in with his controller.

"I'll see you later." I sigh and head toward the front door, not daring to look back at him before making my way through it.

I'm barely down the long walkway to the street when I hear the door close again and Sunshine softly touches my elbow.

"Wait up. You don't have to leave. I thought you wanted to grab something to eat?"

"I don't think that's a good idea." I turn to face him. "You were right. This isn't fair. I can't give you what you want and it's not fair for me to put you through this."

"Come on Mia, I didn't mean it like that."

"It's okay, really. I don't want to hurt you, and I can't lose you as my friend."

"You're not hurting me and you're not losing me. I want you in my life in any way that I can have you. I'm sorry, okay? That was too far." He moves my thumb from my mouth again, holding on to it for a moment before letting it go. "Come back inside, read your book, and I'll order us some food, okay?"

My thumb has been replaced with biting the inside of my cheek as I contemplate his offer, which prompts Sunshine to run his thumb along it softly. I'm internally cursing at myself for both loving his touch and craving more of it. And fuck, for leaning into it. He leads me back to the house after I offer him a small smile. I return to the window seat with a blanket and pillows to support my back, flipping my book back open, while Sunshine makes a call to the local Chinese place. I swear over the past few months he must've memorized everything I like from every restaurant because he's writing my order on a piece of paper and holding it up for my confirmation as he gives his address to the person on the phone. I offer him a thumbs up and force myself to focus on *A Perfect Lie*. So far the heroine has concocted this entirely separate life to cover up something I've not discovered yet. Now she's just met a man who she doesn't feel like she can fully trust, but wants to anyway. Damn, Krista. Way to read right into my soul.

When the food arrives, I join Sunshine on the couch and he flips to a movie channel where some movie plays as background noise. We sit side by side, legs touching, and eat in silence.

"You excited for rehearsals to start next week?" I ask.

"Yes! Though my free time is about to completely disappear," he laughs. "Did you listen to it yet?"

"I think I've decided I want to be surprised. Heathers is one of the few musicals I haven't listened to and I want to go into it with no expectations."

He lets out another small laugh and shakes his head, clearly enjoying some inside joke that I am not a part of. A few more moments pass in comfortable silence as I look around the open space.

"You know, if I could steal your window seat and transplant it to my apartment, I would."

"You're literally the only one who uses it anyways. Feel free to use it whenever, even if I'm not here. What are you reading this time?"

"It's a new thriller by Krista Sayer. She's my favorite by far and she writes the *best* thrillers. They always have the sneakiest plot twists that leave you thinking 'what the fuck just happened.' I think my favorite one by her is *Dreams*. It was about a man who-" Why the fuck am I talking about this? Clearly he's not a reader as evidenced by the lack of books everywhere. He doesn't care about this shit. "Sorry. Never mind."

"A man who what? I have to know now!"

He's smiling at me, waiting for me to continue and it pulls at my heart-strings. I go into detail about the book and his reactions are adorable. At first I think that he's humoring me, but the shock on his face when I reveal the biggest plot twist isn't something anyone could fake. He asks more about my favorite books and it's like word vomit. I can't stop talking about these damn books that I've loved for so long.

Once we've finished eating and cleaning up, I return to my seat at the window. I am about halfway through the book as the sun sets on my face through the window. I only realize that I fell asleep when I feel Sunshine scoop me up and put me on a bed.

I wake in a room I don't recognize but is decorated in a way that makes me think it's a guest room. Surely it would have more than a bed, dresser, and mirror if it was actually someone's bedroom.

The smell of bacon and pancakes fill my nose as I pad into the kitchen, stretching in a silent yawn.

"You're up early," I say to Sunshine's back, causing him to flinch before turning to face me.

Fuck, his bedhead is sexy. I just want to run my fingers through it and-

"Oh, hey." He cuts my thought off by offering me the most gorgeous, dimpled smile. "You passed out in your little book nook last night and I didn't want to wake you to drive home, so I figured the least I could do is make you breakfast. Let's see we've got eggs, waffles, bacon, potatoes, and biscuits."

"How many people are you feeding?" I laugh.

"I wasn't sure what you'd be in the mood for so I made a little bit of everything." He shrugs.

If there's one thing I've learned over the past few months of knowing Sunshine, it's that he is *not* a morning person. Yet here he is, up at eight in the morning having already started on making me breakfast.

"Well then I want to try a little bit of everything. Thank you so much."

Oh, I'm definitely in trouble.

8

Skye had *tried* to warn me. Hell, some could even argue that Sunshine tried to warn me when he'd asked me what I knew about the show. And when Aubrey told me she was playing *Heather* in a musical called *Heathers,* forgive me if I assumed that *she* was playing the female lead instead of *Shannon Murphy.* Shannon Murphy. The same red head that caught up with Sunshine last semester after he was finished walking with me. The same red head I never allowed myself to ask about. The same red head that is currently *grinding* against him. Safe to say I am not the biggest fan of Shannon Murphy. I clear my throat quietly and try to stay mindful about what my face is doing, but I can feel the heat rising to my cheeks. The jealousy I felt last semester, before I knew him and it was Aubrey under him, was child's play compared to what I'm feeling now. I force myself to take quiet deep breaths and focus on the show. Skye nudges me with her elbow next to me. We're not even through the first act yet, and the relationship between Sunshine and Shannon's characters barely just started.

By intermission, I've bloodied three of my fingers from biting on the cuticles while Skye goes on and on about Aubrey's character and how hot she looks.

By the end of the show, I'm fuming with jealousy... even if Sunshine's character *did* die. Fuck. Am I that in over my head that even someone acting alongside Sunshine makes my blood boil?

"What did you think?" Skye asks after we return to the apartment and slump down on the couch.

"It was good! The fact that Sunshine can play a sociopath so well is just a little bit concerning," I laugh. "I was surprised to see Aubrey as Heather and not Veronica though."

"She actually went for Heather. She wanted her last role to be something more fun and sexy."

"I don't know man, Veronica had some pretty... risqué parts herself." I say, recalling her on top of Sunshine.

I don't know if Skye can physically *see* the jealousy on my face, but she must be able to at least sense it with the way she's smiling at me.

"Shannon is *great*, isn't she?" She taunts.

"She's fine. Maybe a little pitchy here and there." I shrug.

Pettiness has never been my thing, and yet here we are.

"Oh *come on*, Mia. Out with it already! You've been trying, and failing by the way, to hide the fact that you like Sunshine for *months* now. When are you just going to give in and let yourself be completely enamored by him?"

"Ugh," I groan, falling on to the couch. "You're right. You're totally right. I feel like a crazy person! I just like him so much and I want him so much and-! Fucking Shannon Murphy riding him on stage. I swear I wanted to pull her off of him by her hair."

"Yes, bitch! Finally!" Skye exclaims excitedly. "Tell me more!"

"I just want to constantly run my hands through his curls, and just be around him all the time. I want to wrap my legs around him and kiss him, and I don't know? Lick his face? Is that weird?" I laugh and Skye joins in.

"Awww my bestie is growing up!" Skye wraps me up in a hug, prompting a laugh and an eye roll.

All this time I've been so worried when it comes to Sunshine. Worried about our friendship, worried about hurting each other...but it's more clear now than ever that we're already in too deep. Being with Sunshine was always inevitable. What is the point in not giving into this when we will both clearly be destroyed by each other either way?

"I have to tell him. Soon." I exhale. "But I feel like at this point I need to do it in like a special way? He's waited all this time. Oh god- what if he's done waiting and wants to move on."

"Nope. None of that. We're not going all twisty-spirally today. That man still wants you today as much as he did when he first met you. Just-ooh! Tell him when we all go out next weekend! So you don't have to focus on finals and telling someone you're obsessed with them at the same time!" Skye jests and I push her playfully.

Can I do this? Can I just come right out and say it?

As if sensing we're talking about him, my phone buzzes with a text from Sunshine.

> Where were you after the show? I figured you'd come back stage and stroke my ever growing ego. ;)

Damn it. The last thing I want is for him to think I don't care. Truth is, I wasn't thinking straight after the show, and I didn't want to meet his stepdad and sister while I was pissed off that another girl was grinding against him.

> I started not feeling great, so I left. Sorry :(

> Oh no! Can I bring you anything to help you feel better?

Fuck. I don't want to lie to him. I mean, it's true— I wasn't feeling great, just not in a sick way.

> That's really sweet of you, but I'll be okay. You were amazing, as always. I'm sorry I won't be able to catch the rest of the shows. Work sucks.

> No worries! I'm just glad you came to one of them. I hope you enjoyed it. Goodnight, Mia.

I *did* enjoy it, even if I got jealous. That man is going to be on Broadway someday, and if he's not then I'll have a lot of questions. His rendition of "Freeze Your Brain" was phenomenal.

"Earth to Mia," Skye waves her hand in front my face. "Parker just texted me and asked me if he should bring you some chicken noodle soup?"

I show her our text thread and she coos.

"See?" She shouts, "I told you he still wants you. Dude just had an amazing performance and wanted *you* to congratulate him. Noticed when *you* weren't there. Wanted to bring *you* soup when you said you didn't feel good. He's just as obsessed as you are."

I hope that's true, but telling him is the only way to know for sure.

"Oh! Aubrey owes me twenty dollars! I told her you guys would end up getting together before the end of the summer!"

"Okay, one— we're not together yet. And two— you're taking bets on my love life?" I feign offense.

"Girl, I *told* Aubrey before you moved here that you and Parker would end up together. Even when you were with James, when I first met Sunshine I thought to myself 'Mia would *love* this man.' Of course, I couldn't say anything because your douchebag of an ex wouldn't let you talk to me for more than five minutes at a time."

I wince at the reminder. James hated when I talked on the phone to anyone, but especially when I spoke to Skye. She hadn't exactly been quiet about the fact that she wasn't James' biggest fan, and naturally he didn't want me to be friends with her because of it.

"I can't believe I ever let a *guy* get between us. Especially someone like James. He really did suck, didn't he?"

"Good for you and bad for him— nothing can ever separate us. I'm so glad that you're *finally* allowing yourself to be happy." Skye gushes.

Hopefully she's right.

9

"You're coming out to celebrate tonight, right?" Sunshine asks as I take my seat to take my last final of the semester, ASL.

"Yeah." I nod and smile at him. "I still can't believe Skye and Aubrey are graduating."

In between classes and work, I've spent most of my time with Sunshine either at my house studying, or in my "little book nook" as he likes to call it. We've also started doing group dinners with Skye and Aubrey, which feels an awful lot like double-dating— not that I'm complaining at this point.

Despite being there often, I've barely talked to either of Sunshine's roommates. Justin's got a sort of boyish charm mixed with a kind of fuck-boy energy. He has short brown hair that's typically spiked up with hair gel, tattoos all down both of his slim arms, and a lip ring. He's short compared to Sunshine, but still towers over me, and he's stick thin.

Asher is definitely the more reserved of the two. He's got shaggy blonde hair and is on the huskier side. He and Justin have been neighbors and best friends since grade school.

They hang out for our group dinners sometimes with their girlfriends, but they don't come around very often. I often wonder how close they are to Sunshine, or if they're just guys to share rent with.

I've studied so much for my finals this semester, I will be surprised if I end with anything less than straight As. So I deserve to go out on the town just for tonight, maybe drink a little, definitely dance a lot, and just have *fun*. After all, I only have until the end of summer before Skye moves in with Aubrey and I have to find somewhere else to live.

Skye, of course, has to dress me up for tonight. She's been trying different clothing combinations on me almost daily for the past few days until she settled on the hot pink dress that fits at the waist and then flares out accompanied with strappy black heels. Eyeing myself in the mirror, I look absolutely ridiculous. Not to mention the fact that I can *barely* walk in heels. I mentally remind myself that this is for Skye, not me. At least she's stayed true to her word and applied minimal makeup.

"Come on, Mi! Sunshine and the guys are already there and waiting for us! Our ride is almost here." Skye urges me from the next room.

Taking a settling breath, I reach for the door handle and walk into the front room. Skye and Aubrey look phenomenal as always and Skye catcalls me as I enter the room. I roll my eyes and follow them out the door.

When we successfully pass the aloof bouncer at the door, I take a seat at a sticky high top table Sunshine snagged along with Skye and Aubrey. Asher and Justin are seated at the table as well with their girlfriends, Kimmy and Becca, respectively. I'm so grateful for the semester to be over and to have a few weeks break to just relax before the summer semester starts. I can't remember the last time I drank, especially in public, so I'm actively reminding myself to take it slow as Aubrey rounds the table with a tray of shots and tall drinks. Fuck. She slides a shot in front of each of us and then holds hers up, the universal signal for us all to follow suit.

"Cheers, bitches! Here's to the end of finals week! Hope you studied, because there's nothing you can do about it now!"

Everyone clinks their shots together before downing it. The sweet burn of the jolly rancher shot hits the back of my throat in the best way possible. As Aubrey passes out each of our drinks, I take in Sunshine across from me. I could've sworn he was watching me a second ago, but he's looking down the table at Skye chattering on about some final now. My body tingles with warmth from the shot and the Long Island Iced Tea that I've somehow already drank half of. I'm keenly aware of the fact that I'm staring at him and yet I can't keep myself from it. He glances back my way and smiles when I continue to stare.

I have to tell him.

"What?" He laughs.

"You're not going to scold me for drinking?" I ask loudly, making sure he can hear me over the loud music.

"We're not at my house," he says with a shrug. "So I'm not going to jail for you."

I sip on my straw, still watching him, and intake air. So much for taking it slow. I slip off of my stool and make my way to the bar to order another drink. My legs are shaky but I'm feeling *good*. As I stand at the bar, trying desperately to get the bartender's attention, I see a pair of familiar hands land on the bar on either side of me, caging me in, before feeling the heat from his body on my back.

I have to tell him.

"Excuse me," Sunshine calls to the bartender, who promptly makes her way toward us with a flirty smile.

I can't blame her though. I've watched women bend to Sunshine's every will for months just for giving them a friendly smile or a wave. It's like he's got some kind of spell on the entire population of straight women.

"A long island iced tea and water, please." He gives her a big smile and she blushes.

I turn to face him, keenly aware of how close I am, and look up at him.

"You tapping out already?" I tease, and he smiles down at me.

"Just making sure you pace yourself."

He puts a twenty dollar bill on the bar before grabbing both drinks and handing me the water first, not breaking eye contact. I take the water from his hands and move my mouth toward the straw, silently daring him to be the first to look away, until I miss the straw and end up awkwardly searching for it with my mouth before I finally have to look down. Fucking smooth. He wears a cocky grin as he leans in and whispers "I win" before putting a hand on my back to guide me back toward the table. All of the girls are already on the dance floor, leaving Sunshine and I alone with Justin and Asher, who are already engaged in conversation. Rather than take my seat across from him, I follow Sunshine to his seat. When he sits, he turns to face me with his legs spread apart and his chin resting on the palm of his hand. I step in between his legs to close the distance between us.

I have to tell him.

"What are you even drinking?" I ask and bring his glass to my lips, taking a drink of the clear liquid before he has a chance to answer.

I had previously assumed it was tequila or rum or maybe even vodka, so I'm surprised when the cool water hits my tongue. He's wearing an amused smile when I look back up at him.

"Someone has to make sure we all get home safely."

"Responsible as always." I roll my eyes and take my drink from him. "Here I was looking forward to seeing you get a little more than tipsy."

"In due time, I'm sure." He laughs.

We're silent for a moment, nodding our heads to the music, and I catch him watching me drink again.

I have to tell him, damn it!

"You'd go to jail for me." I smile knowingly at him.

"Yeah probably." He nods.

"You like me," I state.

I'm getting just a little too cocky but I swear I'd be the cockiest person in the world twenty four seven if it always produced the beautiful smile he's wearing, both dimples indenting the sides of his face.

"I do." He nods again. "But you already knew that."

I step just a bit closer to him, so my thighs are touching the stretch of his jeans.

"You can have literally any other girl that you want. Why keep waiting around?"

"I don't want anyone else." He shrugs.

"Then why haven't you done anything about it?" I ask, taking another sip of my drink.

"The ball is in your court, Mia. You said you wanted to be friends."

My heart is racing as his hand travels lightly up and down my upper arm, causing my stomach to do a backflip.

Now.

"What if I said that I wanted you to kiss me now?" I breathe, placing my drink down on the table and wrapping my arms around his neck.

He pauses a moment, licking his lips as if he's contemplating, before letting out a quiet chuckle, running a hand over his mouth and looking up at the ceiling.

"I'd say you're drunk."

I swear my heart falls into my stomach as I take a step back from him. Logically, I know he's not rejecting me forever but just at this moment. Emotionally, the rejection stings like hell. Why did I drink so much? Why didn't I tell him *weeks* ago?

"You know it's not like that Mia." He playfully rolls his eyes, grabbing my elbow and guiding me back toward him. "If alcohol weren't part of the equation right now, nothing would be stopping me from kissing you. I just don't want to do something you'll regret in the morning, okay?"

I can feel tears sliding down my cheeks as I nod. Fuck, pull it together woman! Sunshine wipes the tears away with his thumbs before he pulls me into a tight hug, swallowing my whole body with his as I stand in front of him.

"Come on, let's go dance," he says, his breath hot against my ear before interlacing his fingers with mine.

He leads me to the dance floor where Skye screeches and pulls me toward her, Aubrey, Becca, and Kimmy. The music is loud, but I can't keep from dancing with them. Sunshine's rejection is still simmering, but it's being overtaken by the thought of him finally kissing me. Damn do I want that. I can feel him watching me, so I might as well put on a show. I twirl about the dance floor, shaking my ass and screaming the lyrics to the song with Skye. Aubrey hands me another Jolly Rancher shot and I down it after clinking it against hers and Skye's. A hand lands on my waist, the goosebumps giving a clear indication of who it belongs to. How the hell does my body know it's him before I even get a chance to see him? He grabs the empty shot glass from my hand and replaces it with a glass of water.

"Please drink more water. I don't want you to have a hangover tomorrow."

His arm wraps around to the front of my stomach, giving me a hug, before walking off again. Why does he have to be so damn *sweet* all the time?

After dancing for what feels like forever, we head back to the table where Sunshine is sitting. More than half of our group has already left for the night, leaving just Skye, Aubrey, Sunshine, and myself. I walk straight to Sunshine and lay my head on his shoulder, tired from all of the dancing.

"Where are the guys?" I ask.

"They're leaving for Michigan in the morning, so they went home to get some sleep."

"I'm about ready to leave, too." Aubrey yawns.

As we head to the door, I'm unsteady until I feel Sunshine's hand on my lower back, guiding me. When I trip over my own feet, he slides his arm around my waist, holding me up. The feeling of him holding me has me practically walking on air. His fingers across my hip is all I can concentrate on until he kisses the side of my head and I swear I turn into a puddle of mush.

"I have a secret," I whisper, turning my head slightly, and he bends over slightly to hear me better.

"What's that?"

"I want more. With you."

I see a hint of shock in his expression before he smiles it away. I'm learning quickly that it is hard to be sexy while wasted.

"It's not the alcohol, I promise. I've been thinking about it for a while now."

"Let's talk more about it tomorrow, okay?"

Sunshine opens my door and wraps his arms around me in a hug before helping me inside.

Once we're on the road to the apartment, I watch as Sunshine hands Skye his phone to choose the music. Skye chooses "I Will Follow You Into the Dark" by Death Cab for Cutie. I keep my eyes focused on the road next to us as I stare out the window. Sunshine is, of course, singing along. I swear there's not a song out there that he doesn't know. I feel his hand stroke the hair on the side of my head and turn to look at him, my head still resting on the headrest.

He offers a soft smile as he sings. I turn my whole body toward him in the car and watch as he continues to sing, his focus returned to the road. I'm fading into sleep when I feel his hand rest on my forearm and smile.

When we get to the apartment, Sunshine opens my door for me. I stumble getting out of the car, but he catches me.

"You're so *nice* to me." I gush, resting my head on his shoulder, "Why are you so *nice*?"

"You're easy to be nice to," he speaks into my hair and wraps his arm around my waist to steady me again.

When we get to the apartment the door is cracked open slightly, and I look up at Sunshine, whose face has turned dark and concerned.

"Did you guys forget to shut the door?" He asks.

"No," I shake my head, "I locked it for sure."

"It's probably just maintenance." Skye stumbles forward but Sunshine stops her.

"At one in the morning? Stay here." He tells us and slowly goes into the apartment.

"Call the cops!" I hear him call from inside. I quickly pull my phone out and dial 911, immediately giving the address to the dispatcher.

"Sunshine?" I call into the apartment and hear rustling.

"Here, you talk to them." I hand the phone to Aubrey and rush inside.

I rush past the trashed common areas and make my way to my bedroom, where I find them. Sunshine is mid-swing toward someone dressed in all black with a black ski mask on. I thought that was only a thing in movies. I watch, breathlessly and unable to move as Sunshine lands a punch to the guy's jaw right before the guy lands a punch to Sunshine's eye, causing me to gasp. Sunshine looks over at me, panic crossing his face. In the split second that he's distracted, the guy punches him again, square in the mouth, and makes his escape through the window. Sunshine throws his hand to his mouth and looks from the window to me.

"Damn it! I told you to stay outside." He snaps, pulling his hand away from his mouth, revealing a brutal split in his lip that's pooling blood. His eye is already starting to swell. I cover my mouth at the sight and tears fill my eyes.

"I'm so sorry."

"No, no." He rushes over to me and wraps an arm around my waist, quickly ushering me toward the outside. "Not your fault."

He leads me outside quickly and looks around the parking lot, but the guy is nowhere to be found. We hear wheels of a car skidding on the pavement and turn our heads to see a sleek black car speeding off.

Sunshine repeats something to himself over and over again under his breath, as he pulls his phone out and walks back to his car. I hear sirens.

"Okay Mia, listen, drink this." He walks back to me and hands me a bottle of water. "I don't want you going to jail tonight on top of this. Just let me talk to the police. Stay calm. I'm right here, okay?"

He hands me a few pieces of gum and I chew them. Two police cars pull up and I feel my heart start to race and my breath quicken.

"Deep breaths, Mia. You can do this. Deep breaths." Sunshine squeezes my hand by my side.

"Good evening, we got a call about a break in. I'm Officer Bant and this is Officer Klum." Officer Bant steps forward and Sunshine moves toward him.

"Yes sir, we just got home and the door was open. I went inside and there was a guy in my girlfriend's room. We got into it and I was trying to keep him here until you guys got here, but he got away from me. I'm pretty sure I have his license plate number here," Sunshine explains, pulling his phone back out.

I'm partially hiding behind Skye, who is now holding my hand. I'm still pretty drunk, but that didn't keep me from hearing the word girlfriend leave Sunshine's lips. My cheeks get hot as Officer Klum walks past me and into the apartment.

"Was anyone else hurt?" Officer Bant asks.

"No officer, I told the ladies to stay outside while I went in," he says.

"You should have called us when you saw the door open."

"Yes sir, I apologize. I just wanted my friends to be safe."

Okay, now it's friends. Am I his friend, or his girlfriend? Was I *that* drunk tonight that I don't remember having that conversation? I'll have to remember to ask him, but I'd be lying if I said I wasn't dying to hear him call me his girlfriend again.

"Do you need an ambulance?"

"I'm alright, just a little banged up. I don't need an ambulance."

"The place is trashed," Officer Klum flippantly announces as he walks out of the apartment and tears sting in the corner of my eyes.

"Alright, we'll take some statements and write up a report, then you can file a claim with your insurance agency," Officer Bant states.

"We, uh, we don't have renter's insurance." Skye says, sheepishly.

"Well, I bet after tonight you will!" Officer Klum laughs and the muscles in Sunshine's jaw tighten at his remark.

"Sir, it's late. Can we come by the station tomorrow to give statements? I've got a place the ladies can stay at for tonight and I think we're all pretty shaken up," Sunshine asks.

"We really prefer to get statements as soon as possible after an event like this to keep details fresh," Officer Bant states.

"Well, I'm really the only one who saw anything. Can we let the girls go get some rest? I'm sure they don't want to stay here knowing it was just ransacked."

"No!" I panic, grabbing his arm. "I don't want to go without you."

The words are out of my mouth before I realize I'm saying them. But I mean it. I don't want to be without him right now. I'm fucking terrified.

"Okay, okay." Sunshine puts his arm around me and kisses the side of my head. "You're not going anywhere. You'll stay here with me."

Officer Bant looks from me to Sunshine and back to me.

"Here's my card. Call me in the morning to come in to give a statement. Poor thing is shaking. Ladies, we're going to take a look around your apartment and take some photos and we'll lock it up when we're finished. You should be grateful that your friend here grabbed his license plate. We've got a pretty good chance of catching the guy with that. Try to get some rest tonight and we will talk in the morning. We'll need statements from all of you."

"Thank you, Officer. We will call first thing in the morning and we will all come up to the station."

Sunshine takes the card and leads me to the car, opening my door and buckling me in.

"How bad was it, Parker?" Skye asks as we get in the car.

"He was in my room," I whisper, pulling my knees to my chest. "He touched my things, he looked at god knows what, and he was *in* my *room*."

I'm not even sure that I said that out loud until I see Sunshine glance over at me and place his hand on my arm. I try to wrap my head around what just happened. I locked the door. I *know* I locked the door. There was someone in our apartment. I close my eyes and try to remember walking through there in search of Sunshine. The couch cushions were scattered throughout the living room and torn open. The dining table was laying with one leg bent inward. I try to picture what my room looked like, but I can't. I was too focused on Sunshine and making sure he was okay. Who would do this? And why?

"Parker, how *bad* was it?" Skye urges again.

"It wasn't great!" Sunshine snaps, "Please, just let me get you guys to my house and we can talk about it in the morning. We all need rest."

"Come on, we can handle it," Skye pushes.

"Jensen, you may be able to, but look at Mia. She's fucking hyperventilating for crying out loud. Now can you please just stop so I can get us there in one piece?"

"He was in my room," I repeat, and Sunshine runs his free hand up and down my arm.

I don't know how long we were in the car or when we got to Sunshine's house. All I know is he carried me inside and laid me on the couch. I feel sick to my stomach. I can't tell if it's the alcohol or anxiety, but I'm definitely going to puke.

"Sunshine, I need a bucket." I whisper, gathering up all the strength I can muster to try and sit up while the room around me spins.

No one responds. Skye is sitting on the opposite couch and Aubrey is next to her, holding her and talking in a hushed voice. Sunshine is pacing from the kitchen to the living room and back, looking down at his phone while he does.

"Bucket," I say a bit louder and Sunshine rushes over to my side, running a hand over the hair on the side of my head.

"What was that?" He asks.

"Buc-"

Too late. I've puked all over his rug and barely missed him.

"Okay, okay. It's okay." He pulls my hair back with one hand and rubs my back with the other. "Hey Aubrey, there's a bucket in that hall closet there, can you grab it for me, please?"

It just keeps coming and Aubrey holds the bucket out for me while Skye attempts to clean the rug. Sunshine keeps rubbing my back.

"It's okay, it'll be over soon," he whispers, "You're okay. Don't worry about the rug, Skye. I'm just going to chuck it. It's old anyways."

"I'm so sorry," I sob in between puking.

"Hey, no, don't be sorry," he croons. "It's just a rug. You're safe and that's all that matters."

I hear Justin and Asher come down the stairs and Aubrey starts talking with them.

"Come on, let's get you a shower," Sunshine says and pulls me into a standing position, his arm around mine to support me. "Skye, can you come help me in the bathroom?"

Skye follows behind us.

"I'm so sorry," I cry, "I'm so sorry."

I look at Sunshine and his black eye is swelling. His lip is busted and bloody. I cry harder. This is all my fault.

"You need to get some ice on that Parker," Skye says.

"First things first," he replies, and sits me on the toilet seat, squatting down in front of me.

"Skye is going to help you get a shower and get some clean clothes on. I'm going to go get some of my clothes from my room and I'll come right back down, okay?" He asks and I grip his forearm.

"Please don't leave," I nearly beg, and I hate how pathetic it sounds.

"Okay, okay." He leans out the door and calls out to Asher to grab some of his clothes from his dresser. "I'll be right here, okay? I'm just going to turn around to give you some privacy but I'm right here."

I lift my arms when Skye gestures for me to once Sunshine is facing the door and she helps me undress.

"I'm sorry," I cry.

"What are you apologizing for?" She asks, "You didn't do anything."

"If I didn't get so drunk, you wouldn't have to take care of me," I cry.

"I'm sorry, exactly how many times have you taken care of me when I was drunk and miserable? Too many. We're all here for you." She says and she starts to wash my hair. I'm so embarrassed and I feel like a child.

"You're not alone in this, Mia. You're safe," Sunshine says, his body still facing the bathroom door.

"No more crying," Skye says, wiping my tears.

"Are *you* okay?" I ask her, trying to calm myself down.

"Well I definitely don't want to go home any time soon, but I'm fine. I'm definitely not nearly as drunk as you are. But yeah man, holy shit someone broke in. That's nuts." Skye says.

"Jensen," Sunshine scolds and Skye rolls her eyes.

I use a washcloth and wash my body before turning off the water. Skye holds the towel out for me and I wrap myself up in it. Sunshine opens the door and leads me by my lower back to the attached guest room where a pair of boxers, sweats, and a t-shirt wait for me on the bed.

"We'll go buy you some clothes tomorrow to keep here." He rubs my back and leads me to the bed.

"Okay," I cry, "I'm so sorry."

"Don't be sorry. Just worry about feeling better," he says and turns his back to me, facing the door to give me privacy again.

I'm slow to get dressed with Skye's assistance as the room continues to feel like it's spinning and I feel nausea rising again.

"Bucket," I say, moving my hand to my mouth.

"We need a bucket in here!" Skye yells and Aubrey rushes in with the bucket.

Sunshine is at my side again in an instant and pulls my hair back before the last bit of my stomach contents empty into the bucket and I'm dry heaving. I swear, I'm never drinking again.

"I think I'm good," I say.

Sunshine hands me a tissue, so I wipe my mouth and offer him a soft smile.

"Let's get you to bed," he says and pulls the covers back on the spare bed.

I shake my head rapidly.

"Mia, it'll be better for you to sleep this off," he says.

"I don't want to be away from you," I panic.

I sound needy, and I am. I just can't imagine being away from him right now. Skye will always be my best friend and I love her but it's just *different*. Sunshine is... secure. Safe.

"Alright." He nods "Jensen, you and Aubrey can sleep in here. I'm going to empty out this bucket and bring Mia up to my bed. Stay right here for just a minute so I can wash this out and then I'll take you upstairs."

Sunshine gathers some supplies— the rinsed out bucket, several water bottles, ice packs, and a bottle of pain killers— and I follow him every step up the way like a lost puppy until we're in his room upstairs.

As often as I've been here, I've never actually been inside Sunshine's room. He has a giant picture of what looks like a set of lungs made up of flowers hanging above a desk in one corner of the room. On top of his desk, he has a binder that looks like it's full of playbills and many scattered papers. Two guitars hang on the opposite wall, and in the middle of the room is a giant, king sized bed with a metal headboard and footboard. In another corner sits a grey, round sofa chair. I don't know what I expected his room to look like, but it wasn't this. It's tranquil and artistic and embodies Sunshine perfectly.

I follow him to his attached bathroom and he opens a drawer, pulling out a new toothbrush package.

"I always keep spares. Do you want to try to brush your teeth?" He asks and I nod, grateful that he seems to always think of everything.

His bathroom is just as nice as the rest of the house. A double vanity is set up one wall with a whirlpool tub on the other, and a separate shower in the corner.

"How have you hidden this from me?" I ask, grazing my fingers on the tub and he laughs, putting toothpaste on a toothbrush for me and then on his own.

We brush our teeth side by side and I take in his injuries in the mirror. His eye is still swollen, and his lip is split open. He tries to hide it, but I watch as he gingerly moves around the it, the toothpaste probably stinging the open skin.

"Is this weird?" I spit and ask, "Me sleeping in your room?"

"No," he says. "I'll sleep on the sofa, and you can have the bed. How are you feeling?"

"I don't know," I say with a shrug. "I'm not going to throw up again if that's what you're asking."

"It's not, but good to know." He smiles at me and it causes his lip to start bleeding again.

I grab some toilet paper and dab it dry, my eyes filling with tears as guilt tears at my heartstrings.

"I'm okay," he says, grabbing my wrist gently. "Bruises and cuts heal."

When we retreat to his room, I crawl into the bed and curl the blankets around myself as Sunshine moves some pillows around on the sofa before grabbing an extra blanket from his closet. When he turns the lights out a few minutes later, the room is silent and pitch black. I can't remember the last time I was afraid of the dark, but I am now. If I look around, I see nothing. If I close my eyes, all I can see is that douchebag hurting Sunshine. I feel tears slide down my cheek and fuck, I am so tired of *crying*.

"Sunshine?" I whisper into the darkness after several minutes of trying to calm myself.

"Yeah? You okay?" he whispers back.

"No," I cry. "I'm scared. Would... is it weird if I ask you to come lay with me?"

He doesn't answer and just slides in bed next to me, not making contact with me the way I so desperately need. I know it's not fair to him, and I'm not sure how this will change our relationship, but I scoot closer to him and lay my head on his chest. I'm pleasantly surprised as he wraps his arm under me and pulls me closer to him. I take a deep breath, inhaling the clean and woodsy scent that I have come to love, and finally feel some of the tension leave my body. While he strokes my hair, I focus on his breathing.

"Is this okay?" I whisper and I feel him nod his head against mine. "Are you okay?"

"This?" He asks, giving me a gentle squeeze. "This is perfect. And I will be fine. Sleep. I've got you."

I try to focus on the rise and fall of his chest rather than my heart beating at an insanely fast rate. I'm scared and tears are silently falling down my cheek and onto Sunshine's shirt. That's when he starts singing "Lean On Me" by Bill Withers. I close my eyes and focus on the words he's singing, letting sleep take hold of me quickly.

When I wake in his arms, everything feels like it'll be okay. Like no matter what happened last night, I'm good.

"We need to go up to the station and give statements." Sunshine stretches and mumbles out through a sleepy haze.

I groan and throw a pillow over my face.

"I know, it sucks, but on the bright side we can come back here after. Maybe watch some movies? Or you can read? Go for a swim?" He smiles.

"Where are we going to go?" I ask. "Skye and me, I mean."

"We'll cross that bridge when we come to it. For now you can stay with me. I told Skye and Aubrey they could stay in the spare room, but I don't know that they've decided on anything yet. After we get done at the police station, we'll head over to the store to get you some clothes."

"Thank you," I say. "Truly, I don't know what I did to deserve this."

He offers a small smile and peels his shirt off, replacing it with another. I can't help but stare as he does.

"I washed your clothes from last night," he says, gesturing to the dress folded neatly on the sofa chair. "Well, Skye and I both did, I guess. I had her throw them in the washer so I didn't have to leave you. I threw them in the dryer first thing this morning."

"I'm sorry about last night."

"For what?" He asks, sitting up on the bed next to me.

I shrug. Where the hell do I start? I was sorry for getting so uncontrollably drunk that he didn't believe me when I said I wanted to be with him. I was sorry for teasing him. I was sorry for making him sleep in bed with me, knowing just how we feel about each other.

"You called me your girlfriend," I state, changing the subject.

"Uh, what?" he asks.

"To the cops. You said that you saw him in your girlfriend's room."

He turns his face away from me, smiling, and runs a hand over his eyes.

"I'm sorry, Mia," he says. "It just slipped out. I know where we stand and I don't, like, go around telling people that you're-"

I cut him off by putting my hand over his mouth. He's so cute when he's flustered.

"I liked it. I meant what I said last night."

His eyebrows shoot up and I slowly move my hand away from his mouth. He's silent for a minute, just staring at me.

"Believe me when I say that I so desperately want to have this conversation, but you went through a lot yesterday. Let's table it until things have calmed down a little, okay?"

I'm sure I can't hide the disappointment on my face because he runs his thumb along my cheek, cueing me to stop my teeth's assault.

"Don't do that. I still want you just as much, if not more than I did before. I've been dying for you to say that. We just need to focus on helping you through this first, okay?"

I lean into his hand and nod.

10

I don't know who needs to sit down with these officers and explain that the whole "good cop, bad cop" isn't needed in situations like this, but someone should probably tell them. Officer Bant is sweet, understanding, and even sympathetic, while Officer Klum is trying to find any way to blame *us* for the break-in. Axel Halcro. That's who the car is registered to, but the address is vacant, because apparently that's our luck. Officer Klum asked all of us if we knew the name, maybe heard it in passing or if he went to school with us. I'm pretty sure if any of us had ever heard it, we'd recognize the name. Officer Bant tells us that we can go into the apartment at any point and recommends installing an alarm system. As if we'll ever live there again. They're working with the complex to get video footage from the cameras scattered throughout the complex, but they're not sure if it would've covered our apartment. Basically catching this guy is a crapshoot. I'm processing everything they say, but my focus is on the way Sunshine is gently rubbing my back, comforting me the whole time.

"We'll have to go get your cars at some point," Sunshine says as he drives to a local department store. "I don't care to drive you to campus, or let you use my car, but I'm thinking you probably don't want to just let yours sit there."

I nod and look out the window. I still can't believe that someone was in our apartment. I feel so incredibly violated. If I could afford it, I would replace every single thing in that apartment. I don't want anything that guy had his hands on. How am I ever supposed to feel secure again?

"I might go to Aubrey's until we figure out what we're going to do," Skye announces and I look over at her. "We were talking about moving into her place in a few months anyways..."

I knew I was going to have to find somewhere to go for the new semester, but I didn't think it would be so soon. I can't blame her for wanting to live with her girlfriend, especially with graduation this month.

I stand by the cart, completely uninterested in clothes shopping, and watch as Sunshine and Skye pick clothes for me. Skye and Aubrey pick over some items for her as well although she's kept a lot of clothes at Aubrey's apartment as it is.

"Are you okay?" Sunshine asks as we walk toward the intimates section. I shrug and he offers a comforting smile and squeezes my shoulder.

I feel weird being in Sunshine's clothes with these high heels I wore last night. People must think I've got some kind of walk of shame going on.

"Do you need anything else while we're here?" He asks and I shake my head, knowing I have an extra pair of tennis shoes in my car. We head to the checkout line and Skye hugs me from behind, resting her head on my shoulder.

"I'll be right back," Sunshine says. "I need to grab a few things, but I'll be back before it's our turn.

"We have to get the rest of our stuff," she says.

"Yeah, what's left of it." I give a small sarcastic laugh.

"Was it that bad?" she asks.

"I honestly don't remember. I was so focused on making sure Sunshine was okay." I shrug.

"He *is* okay though." She squeezes me tighter.

"Did you see his eye? His lip? How is that okay?" I turn to face her.

"Minor bumps and bruises." She shrugs it off.

"That he wouldn't have gotten if it weren't for me," I whisper.

"Come on, don't do that. Despite that asshole cop's opinion, this wasn't anyone's fault except the guy who broke in. We locked the door."

"If we hadn't gotten so close, it wouldn't have happened," I say, tears filling my eyes.

"Even if you and Sunshine hadn't gotten close, he's one of my friends, too. I still would have dragged both of your asses out to celebrate the end of the term and it still would have happened, only something could have happened to us. We don't know what kind of guy that was. He could have really hurt us," Skye says.

"Please, stop feeling guilty. I wouldn't change anything," Sunshine says, walking over and pulling me into his arms. "Believe me, this is nothing. I've seen way worse."

He gestures to his face.

After we get our clothes, we all pile back into Sunshine's car. I'm disappointed when Skye decides to hang out at Aubrey's apartment for the afternoon, but I understand. This didn't just happen to me, it happened to Skye too. I need to let her process it in her own way. When we get back to Sunshine's house, I'm exhausted and slightly hungover so I head immediately for the couch, determined to nap. Justin and Asher are sitting on the opposite couch, playing some zombie game.

"Hey Mia," Justin says. "How you feeling?"

"I'm okay," I lie. "What are you guys playing?"

"Endless Hour. You want in, Parker?" Asher calls to him in the kitchen.

Sunshine saunters over and I shift to make room for him on the couch. He pats his lap and I move my legs to drape over his. His hand rests on my calf, tracing slow, lazy circles with one finger while his eyes stay fixed on the television.

"Nah, I'll sit this one out."

"Do you want to try, Mia?" Justin dangles a spare controller in front of me.

"Sure, why the hell not?" I shrug and take the controller. "Take it easy on me though, I have no idea what I'm doing."

Sunshine explains the game and the controls to me.

"So basically the same as your other zombie games. Shoot them and don't let them get near me. Got it," I say, and Asher sets it up as a three player game.

I adjust to lie on my back and Sunshine continues to trace circles on my calf. I know he's noticed the goosebumps that arose because he's wearing a small smile, even while he watches us decimate zombies on the tv. Will I always get goosebumps from his touch?

The game is tough. I've never been big into video games unless you count city building games and random app games that never seem to be quite what the ads promise. Sunshine coaches me on where to shoot and I feel like I'm getting the hang of it. I feel like I can breathe. This all feels so normal. Almost like something traumatic *didn't* just happen.

"You're not half bad at this for someone who claims not to play video games," Justin teases, turning the game off after several rounds.

"He's not wrong. You're kind of a natural," Asher agrees.

"When do you guys head out?" Sunshine asks.

"I think we're planning on leaving here soon," Asher says.

"Where are you guys going again?" I sit up on the couch.

"We take our girls home to Michigan every summer. Our parents own lake houses that they hardly ever use, so we stay there and look after the place," Asher responds.

"Yeah, Parker here *used* to go with us, but then he bought the house." Justin teases.

"It wasn't about the house, I've told you guys this. I help out with Birdie in the summer. Someone has to watch her while Adam works," he says.

"Relax, we're just yanking your chain." Asher laughs.

"Wait, you own this place?" I ask and he nods.

Damn. He's got a whole ass mortgage. How did I not know this place was his?

"Skye just texted, she wants to go by the apartment later today to gather some things and talk to the leasing office about moving out. Do you want to go?" Sunshine asks.

"No time like the present, I suppose." I give him a small smile and stand.

~

The asshole must have been here a while before we got to the apartment, because it is absolutely trashed. All of our electronics are broken alongside picture frames, drawers are hanging open... It's like a freaking hurricane came through here.

"Fuck!" Skye says, as we walk into the apartment. "He didn't even take anything, why the fuck would someone break in just to destroy all of our shit? And why the fuck didn't we get renters insurance?"

"We said we didn't need it." I let out a humorless laugh, looking around in disbelief.

Sunshine isn't far behind me as I head to my bedroom to take in the damage. Several blankets lay on the ground, my dresser drawers are on the floor, and clothes are scattered throughout the room. I rub my eyes and pinch the bridge of my nose while Sunshine grabs my suitcase out of my closet.

"We'll make sure to wash these," he says, as he starts packing my clothes. "We can get a storage unit for your furniture while we figure out where you want to live. Though, I think I can find a space in the house for all of it if you wanted to bring it there."

I barely register what he's saying as I run my fingers across the top of my now-broken vanity I've had since I was seven. My mom bought it for me when I started gaining an interest in makeup. Back when she could stand to look at me. I fight back the tears that threaten to spill when I notice that all of my makeup inside is broken.

"Everything will be okay, Mia," Sunshine says. "We can get you a new vanity, we can buy new makeup. These are all things that are replaceable. *You* aren't."

I nod and walk out of the room. I return with a large black garbage bag and start to toss various belongings in from the floor. I'm not sure I want to touch *anything* that douchebag might have had his hands on. My chest tightens and I become acutely aware of the overwhelming feeling of devastation that seems to hit all at once, so I strip a corner of my bedsheets and take a seat.

"Can I just have a minute?" I ask Sunshine.

"Yeah, of course, I'll go check on Skye."

He barely made it out of the room when I put my head in my hands and silently cry, trying to figure out why the hell this happened. Skye is pretty popular with just about everyone she meets, and I haven't been here long enough for anyone to truly hate me. There's plenty of people who don't like me, but they're all a thousand miles away. Plus, none of them know where I live.

After several minutes of quietly crying and trying to calm myself down, I lift my head to take another glance around the room. I never want to come here again, but the thought of packing everything up is so nauseating that there's no way I can do it on my own. When I leave my room, Sunshine is cleaning up some of the trash that's strewn about the apartment. Skye is moving from her bedroom to her car, loading some of her stuff up. I peek in her room and noticed that a lot of it is undisturbed. I guess he must have gotten to my room first.

"Sunshine, can you come help me please? I don't want to come back here and I need help packing what I still want up."

He looks up at me with the garbage bag in hand and nods.

"If you're helping Skye though, it's okay. I can-"

"Nope. I'm all yours." He smiles up at me. God how I need those words to be true.

Sunshine pats the stool to my vanity when we get in the room, gesturing for me to sit. He then starts quietly sorting belongings with direction into either the trash or an empty tote I had in my closet. He inspects several books that I've probably reread more times than is healthy— books whose pages now decorate my floor— and tosses them in the trash bag. His face is somber as he looks at me after nearly each book being tossed in the trash, as if silently apologizing and I swear my heart is breaking. I know it's stupid- I know they're just books and I'm probably being overdramatic, but they were *my* books. With *my* highlights of my favorite phrases. With *my* notes in the margins. After about an hour of sorting through various belongings, Sunshine makes his way to the seemingly untouched boxes in the corner of my room— the same ones that have been staring at me since I moved in. He moves to open the top one when I nearly yell, "Stop!"— causing him to stop mid-movement.

"You can... those are..." I try to find my words. "Honestly I don't know why I still have those. Just toss them."

"You're sure you don't want to go through them before you just throw it all out?"

Both boxes were packed in a rush when I left my apartment with James and marked with large, red duct tape X's. The only thing I remember is I packed them while I was crying and it was full of things I wasn't sure I was ready to part with yet.

"It's all stuff from or to do with James."

Sunshine nods and stays by the boxes, waiting for further instruction. He's looking at me with so much patience and empathy that I'm not even sure he heard me.

"Fuck it," I say, standing and making my way to the boxes.

Sunshine asks if I want him to step out, but I don't. I'm not entirely sure why, but I've been afraid to go through them and it'll be nice to have him by my side through it. The first is filled with gifts I'd received from James: the diamond necklace he gave me after our first date... the jade earrings he gave me after I went down on him the first time... the watch he gave me after our first real fight... This box alone probably has several thousands of dollars in jewelry. I guess it's a good thing I didn't toss them. All of this jewelry that I had once loved and wore often now makes me nauseous at the sight.

"You okay?" Sunshine asks.

"He really knew how to throw his parents money around..." I say with a nod. "Can you... would you sell them for me?"

He responds with a nod and places a comforting hand on my shoulder. When I open the second box, I find it filled with my "memories" box. Inside sits concert tickets, movie ticket stubs, playbills, and letters. Not *all* from James of course— some are from movies I saw with Frankie, or concerts I went to with Skye. I place the small box on top of the tote and take another glance around the room. We've pretty much gone through the entire apartment aside from the larger furniture, so we make our way to the leasing office. They are very apologetic and explain that the guy had somehow avoided all of their cameras. They agree to let us terminate our lease without a fee since their waiting list is so long, and offer to remove all of our unwanted furniture for us given what we'd gone through. Of course they "have to" keep our security deposit for terminating early. All things considered, they're being pretty generous. Skye and I agree and sign the paper, agreeing that we have ten days to vacate any belongings we want to keep and the rest will be trashed. At least we won't have to come back here after today.

"Okay, so what do you want to do?" Skye asks as we walk toward my car. "Aubrey's place is only a one bedroom, but we can maybe look into getting into a two bedroom?"

"Or, you could always stay with me," Sunshine says as he nonchalantly twirls his keyring around his finger.

"What?" I ask.

"I mean, I have the spare room. You wouldn't have to pay rent or any bills or anything." He shrugs.

"What?" I ask again, shocked.

"This way you can still have your own space and you'd be safe. Just give it some thought, no pressure. In the meantime, drive safe," he says, getting into the driver's seat of his car.

Moving in? With Sunshine? Why do I feel like it's both the best and worst idea ever?

I drive in silence back to Sunshine's house, taking in his offer. Outside of Skye and Sunshine, I've made a couple of friends in the education department and at the library, but I wouldn't say I'm close enough to anyone to be their roommate. Skye and Aubrey have been looking forward to moving in together all semester, so there is no way in hell I'm crashing their party. It's either move in with Sunshine, live on my own in a dorm that I'll have to take more loans out for, or get my own apartment... where I'd probably struggle with both paying bills *and* feeling secure.

Wait, am I actually considering this? It would definitely be the easiest choice, but I have to think of how it'll affect our relationship...

When I arrive at the house, Sunshine offers me a smile as he leans against his car, waiting on me.

The sense of normalcy as we enter the house is refreshing. If I'm completely honest with myself, Sunshine's house has felt more like home than the apartment ever did, but I never thought I'd actually be calling it home. But, what if I move in and things don't end up working out. Then I'd be in the same situation I am now, except without one of my best friends. And what about Skye? I can tell she and Sunshine have become close while I was off at Duke... would she *really* side with me if I broke Sunshine's heart?

"I know that look. What are you thinking about?" Sunshine asks as he tosses his keys in the key bowl on the entryway table.

"It's nothing." I wave him off and undo the straps on my shoes, grateful to be barefoot again.

The way he tightens his lips screams that he doesn't believe me, but he also doesn't push it further.

As I'm preparing to make myself comfortable on the couch, I'm stopped in my tracks when I see the window seat. I know a lot has happened and I've been distracted, but how did I not notice this before now?

I walk slowly to it, almost afraid it'll disappear if I get too close. I softly trail my fingers along the new cushion of the now slightly inclined seat and continue until my fingers meet the side of a newly built-in bookshelf that frames either side of the window. Overwhelmed, I slump into the window seat, and look up at Sunshine, who has just been watching me taking it it and now takes a seat next to me. There's a small, insecure part of me yelling that this is just something Sunshine wanted to do and it isn't for me at all, but it's so easy to ignore given that there are several books by well-known thriller and mystery authors, including several books by Krista Sayer.

"When?" I ask, unable to form more words.

"I built it over the past few days. I just thought I'd make it more comfortable for you since you read here so much. Plus I know you hate that your other books are at your mom's house, so I figured at the very least I can let you store some books here."

He *built* me a *bookshelf*. This man, who I've denied myself of for *months* built me a fucking bookshelf. I stand again, taking it all in, when I notice drawers just under the seat. Sunshine follows my gaze and brings his legs up to sit cross-legged as I open the drawers. Inside one drawer is my favorite throw blanket and a small pillow. In the other lies a book journal and an assortment of different colored gel pens along with a big bag of gummy bears and a bag of Flamin' Hot Fritos— my all-time favorite snacks.

"You did this for me?" I ask and he offers a nod.

Before I can think better of it, I make my way to stand in front of him and press my lips to his. He's taken by surprise and pulls back just enough to rest his forehead against mine.

"Are you sure this is what you want?" he whispers and I nod.

"Do you still want me?" I ask, which prompts a soft laugh from him.

"Are you kidding? I've wanted you since the day I met you," he responds, tucking a strand of hair behind my ear.

Running my fingers through his hair, I bring his face to mine and kiss him again, smiling beneath the kiss. He runs his fingers through my hair and pushes the back of my head slightly, as if he can't get close enough, planting his other hand on my waist.

Admittedly I don't have a lot of experience, but I've been kissed before. There was Tommy in the fourth grade back when I still thought boys had cooties— completely unsolicited and pretty gross. Of course, several times with James— they were... fine, I guess. And there was one drunken kiss from Skye a few years back when she thought we were *that* kind of friends. I have to admit that one was pretty nice because obviously I love her and she knows what she's doing, but it made me realize I am most certainly straight. But this? Nothing even comes close to this. His lips are soft and plush and the way he's holding me... I feel like my knees are going to give out. He pulls away slightly and rests his forehead against mine again.

"You have no idea how long I've wanted to do that," he smiles and interlaces his fingers in mine on both hands.

"It was even better than I imagined," I mumble.

"Ah, so you *have* imagined it." He raises his eyebrows suggestively and I laugh.

"Don't make fun of me."

"Never," he says and kisses my forehead.

"I have boundaries. If we're going to live together."

"Wait, you're actually considering it?" He asks, a huge grin overtaking his face as I nod. "I'm a flexible person."

"I take the spare room, like we talked about before... if that's still okay. I'll move my stuff in there," I say.

"Done," he says, shaking his head as if it's the easiest negotiation ever.

"I'm not done. You need to let me pay half of the bills," I say.

"No," he says, shaking his head. "Absolutely not. It's meant to be split between at least three people."

"Okay, but your roommates are gone for the summer and I know you. You probably pay for everything when they go," I say.

He thinks a moment, squinting his eyes at me in scrutiny.

"One bill. You can have the gas bill," he counters.

"The gas bill *and* groceries," I say.

"You buy your groceries and I buy mine."

"That'll be too complicated. I buy all of the groceries."

"But I'm a guy, I eat a lot more than you do," he complains.

"All of the groceries or I find other arrangements."

I stand my ground, completely bluffing. It's not like I have many other options.

"Only until the guys come back in the Fall. Then it's split evenly," he says.

"Then it's *all* split evenly. I pay what they pay," I say and raise my eyebrows at him.

"Fine," he sighs, briefly putting his head down in a dramatic fashion and raising it again. "Anything else?"

"We need to figure out what we're doing. I don't do well in gray areas."

"Sounds like we should go on a date, then."

An actual *date* with Sunshine? Sign me the fuck up. I nod, biting my lip to try not to appear too eager.

"Well then, I have a date to plan. If I know you, and frankly if I know Skye, you should probably go call her." He kisses the side of my head and stands.

I head into what is now my room and take it in. It's not huge but it's bigger than the room in the apartment. The attached bathroom is a nice amenity too. I plop onto my stomach on the king sized bed and as much as I try, I can't erase the smile that's on my face. He likes me. He wants me. And *fuck* he's a good kisser. I literally kick my feet giddily and giggle before pulling up a Facetime call with Skye.

"Hey, is everything okay?" Skye asks as she answers, but then gasps when she sees me. "Wait I know that smile."

"We kissed," I whisper, trying to contain my excitement.

"WHAT!" Her screech is so loud on the other end there is no way Sunshine didn't hear it. I motion for her to quiet herself to avoid the embarrassment. "Aubrey! We're going back to Parker's house!"

I walk out of my room in search of Sunshine and find him sitting at the kitchen table on his computer. When he notices me standing in the living room he turns his attention toward me.

"Do you care if Skye and Aubrey come over?" I ask.

"You live here, Mia. You don't have to ask permission to have friends over."

"I'm sorry, what! You *live* there, too?" Skye yells from the other end of the phone.

I hang up on her quickly and my cheeks burn in embarrassment. Sunshine lets out a quiet laugh and turns back to his computer. I can't help but stare at him as he does. He's wearing a pair of black, thick-rimmed glasses that I've not seen before, and I swear I didn't think he could possibly get sexier. I sit across from him at the table and take in his injuries from last night, guilt tugging at my chest. He closes his laptop and looks over at me.

"Hi." I smile at him.

"You're staring."

"I've never seen you in glasses before."

"Yeah, my contacts were bugging my eyes."

Sunshine watches my every move as I move from my seat and stand in front of him. He's turned in his chair to face me and looks up at me through his glasses while I run my fingers through his curls. I move my hand down the side of his head and rest it against his cheek, feeling the warmth of his soft skin. The feel of his lips as he turns his head slightly to kiss my palm make the butterflies in my stomach go wild, reminding me what his lips felt like on mine and desperately wanting them again. I have to be smart about this. I know if I let myself, my dumbass will dive in head first only to break his heart when I come back up for air. He's too good to hurt with my inability to feel what I'm supposed to feel.

"What's going on in that beautiful mind of yours?" He asks.

"Nothing." I shake my head, offering him a smile.

He's looking at me with skepticism when the front door swings open. Reflexively, I quickly move my arm back to its side. Skye's squeal of excitement echoes through the hallway, earning a small laugh from Sunshine.

"I believe I have a date to plan." He kisses my cheek. "I'll be up in my room if you need me."

Skye and Aubrey walk into the kitchen as Sunshine climbs the stairs to his bedroom.

"Okay, we literally saw you an hour ago. What the hell happened?" Skye practically yells.

"Come on." I laugh and gesture towards my room. "We'll hang out in here."

Skye and Aubrey listen intently as I recount the hour. Skye is practically bouncing with excitement and then throws her arms around me in a hug. When my phone chirps with an incoming text message, Skye reads it over my shoulder.

> Tonight too soon? I can swing by your room and "pick you up" at like 6:30?

Skye snatches the phone out of my hand, smiling like a madwoman and typing, saying the words aloud as she does.

> Yes, 6:30 would be fine. Afterall, I need to let my hair down a little since I work sooooo hard all the time. Looking forward to it, sexy.

"Skye!" I scoff and take my phone back. I start drafting an apology text when another comes through.

> Well damn, here I thought I was texting Mia. Nice to know you have boundaries, Jensen ;) Mia, I'm looking forward to it.

"Okay, it's," Skye checks her phone. "Girl it's five, we need to get you *ready!*"

11

"It's too much," I say, looking in the mirror.

Skye and Aubrey picked out a royal blue spaghetti strap, knee-length dress that hugs just a bit more around the hips than I'd like. My wavy, chestnut hair is slightly messy and my emerald eyes have more makeup on than I'd ever do for myself.

"No, it's not Mia. Come on, you're going out with Sunshine freaking Parker. Do you know how many girls would want to be in your shoes?" Aubrey says and Skye shoots her a jealous look. "Do you know how many *straight* girls would want to be in your shoes?"

Skye smiles when Aubrey corrects herself.

There's a knock on my bedroom door and I feel my heart skip a beat. Aubrey lets out a small, excited squeal as she opens it, revealing Sunshine—smiling and gorgeous as ever. He's wearing a tight black t-shirt under a blue flannel and jeans. His hair is the same sexy, tousled mess and his eyes almost seem iridescent against the color of his shirt. In his hand is a bouquet of brightly colored flowers.

"You look gorgeous." He smiles at me, walks over to me and pulls me into a hug. "These are for you."

"You didn't have to do all this." I roll my eyes, playfully.

"Oh come on Mi, you could use some flowers to brighten up the place!" Skye smiles at Sunshine and basically pushes me toward him. "Have fun you crazy kids!"

"You ready?" he asks and I nod.

"Aubrey and I are just going to hang here so we can hear *all* the details when you get back."

After shaking my head and rolling my eyes again, I follow Sunshine to his car, and he starts driving. The ride is quiet, and I can't stop wiping my sweaty palms on my dress.

Get it together, woman! It's not like we never hang out.

Thankfully we pull up to the Crishner Community Theater before I have a chance to spiral further. The sign in front indicates that there's a performance of "Little Shop of Horrors" playing and I can't help but feel giddy. Not only did he bring me to see a musical, it's also one I haven't seen yet.

I'm still grabbing my purse from the backseat when he rounds the car and opens my door for me. Who does that?

We walk toward the theater side by side, his fingers interlaced with mine. His hand is twice the size of mine and his skin feels so soft aside from the calluses on the tops of his fingers that I can only assume are from the guitars in his room.

Despite being a community production, the musical is amazing. Sunshine holds my hand the whole time and I can't help but steal glances of him throughout. I watch his eyes light up during "Suddenly, Seymour" and smile. When I'm not covertly staring at him, I swear his eyes are on me, too. I hope he can't sense how nervous I am to *finally* be out with him as something other than friends. When it's over, Sunshine stands and holds his hand out for me, keeping me close as we make our way through the crowd to get to the car.

"What did you think?" He asks as we walk outside.

"It was *awesome*. Thank you so much." I smile at him.

"Late dinner?" he asks.

"Sure," I say. "It'll give us a chance to talk."

He opens my car door for me before hopping in the driver's seat. A few minutes later, we pull up to a quaint little Mexican restaurant.

Sunshine asks for a table outside in the empty patio area. At least we'll have a bit of a breeze and some privacy. He pulls my chair out for me before I sit and places a quick kiss on the top of my head when I sit.

"Just wait until you try the food. It's amazing. Probably my favorite Mexican place around here... Queso?"

"If the question is queso, the answer is always yes." I agree and smile.

"So." He smiles at me after a few moments while we wait for the waiter.

"So." I giggle, not quite sure what to talk about.

Usually, when we hang out there's never a shortage of conversation—and if there is, it's only because we're blissfully co-existing, doing our own thing side by side.

The waiter walks over and gives us chips, salsa, and queso. We place our orders and are alone again.

"What are you scared of when it comes to us?" He asks, jumping right in.

I'm scared of hurting you. I'm scared that the more you get to know me, the less you'll actually want to be with me. I'm scared I can't give you what you deserve. I'm scared that you're too good for me, and way out of my league.

Of course, I can't actually say any of that, so I settle for the fear that is most obvious with pretty much any relationship.

"What if we do this and we fail?" I ask.

"That's always the risk, isn't it? But, I think what you should be asking yourself is what if we do this and succeed?"

Ever since I met him, Sunshine has always known the exact right thing to say to calm me down in the middle of an internal spiral.

"Touché." I laugh, taking a chip. "So, what are *you* looking for? What are we doing?"

"What do you want it to be?" He asks.

"No, no, I asked you." I blush.

"What do I want?" He asks, taking both of my hands in his and holding eye contact. I nod. "I want to be with you. I want to hang out with you and hold you and kiss you and tell you over and over again what a spectacular person you are. I want to show you how breathtakingly beautiful you are. I want you to meet my sister and show you off to my friends. I want to be on stage and see you in the audience. I just want you, Mia. In every way I can have you."

"Wait, hold on," I say holding a hand up, "So like, you want me to be your girlfriend?"

"Yes," he laughs and kisses the top of one of my hands. "Yes Mia, I want you to be my girlfriend."

"I want that too," I say, biting my lip before our orders are placed in front of us, interrupting the moment.

"So I have a question," I say once the waiter has left again.

"Shoot," he says, eating.

"Why do you think your Mom named you Sunshine? Like aside from the hippie thing? Is there a reason behind it?" I ask, desperate to change the subject, but also wanting to know everything there is to know about him.

"Well yes there was the *hippie thing*." He laughs. "But she was also fifteen when she had me. She used to sing 'You Are My Sunshine' to me all the time when she was pregnant and after. My dad left before I was even born so it was just us. She had her mom to help sometimes, but she literally had to work up until the day I was born... and then went back to work a week later. She used to tell me that song was made for me, because as long as she had me she was happy."

"Wow, it sounds like she was really strong," I say.

"Oh, she was amazing. The best. She started her own company when I was five and worked her ass off to provide for me. I didn't even know it until I was older. She made sure I needed and wanted for nothing."

His whole face lights up when he talks about his mom, and I feel a mixture of sadness and jealousy. Sadness, of course, because he lost her way too young, but also a tinge of jealousy that he had that kind of relationship with her. I would give anything to have had a mom like that. I wonder if his mom would have liked me. If she would have approved.

"What was her company?" I ask.

"Have you heard of Sunny Soaps? We sell like... soaps and shit." He laughs.

"Wait, you're messing with me, right? That's literally a stop in the mall every time I go. That's hers?"

"Yep! Well it was... it's my step-dad Adam's, Birdie's, and mine now," he says.

"Well damn... you have a mortgage *and* own a business." I laugh. "*Wait.* They're all musical themed titles... that makes so much sense!"

"Yeah." He laughs at my excitement. "My mom was super into musicals, too. I'm honestly not all that involved in the business though. Adam has a better mind for it than I do. Plus, he worked with Mom on it after they got married and especially after she got sick. I just help out making products here and there when needed, and help with naming them... and Birdie just collects the paycheck in an account that she has no access to yet."

"Still, that's so cool," I say.

"What's your favorite product?" he asks.

"I *love* 'Everything is Rosie.'"

"Name that musical," he challenges.

"Come on, give me a challenge at least. It's *Bye Bye Birdie.*" I feign offense.

"Yeah! Damn. I've actually made that one quite a few times. You may have had soap made by me before you even met me." He laughs.

We sit quietly as we eat. He wasn't lying about the food, it's probably some of the best tacos I've ever had. He pays before I have a chance to even look at the ticket, because of course he does. We walk to his car hand in hand and stay that way for the drive home, too. Driving in Sunshine's car and listening to him sing along to the radio has quickly become my favorite activity. Even when he laughs at me for asking to stay in the car until the song is over.

"Thank you so much for a great night out." I say when we reach the front door, knowing damn well that Skye and Aubrey are just on the other side of it waiting.

"Get used to it, because there's many more where that came from."

He tucks a strand of hair behind my ear and leans down to kiss me. I swear when his lips are on mine, it's like fireworks exploding in my chest and my head is swimming with so much affection for him it has to be unnatural. I place my hand on his cheek and pull him closer, deepening the kiss. After a few moments, he pulls away and my stomach drops at the loss of connection. I think I'd be happy to kiss him every moment of every day.

"Come on, let's get inside." He nods toward the door and holds it open for me.

When we walk through the door, Sunshine lets out a small laugh and clears his throat as we see Aubrey straddling Skye's lap on the couch. I swear I've never seen Aubrey move to a standing position faster. Judging by Skye's unruly hair, we either just walked in on a really intense make out session... or the tail end of something more.

"Oh, hey guys!" Skye smiles at us with zero shame and we laugh.

Sunshine gives me a long hug before he leans down to whisper in my ear.

"I'll see you in the morning. Have fun with your friends."

He kisses me on the cheek, offers Skye and Aubrey a wave, and retreats to his room.

"Tell. Me. Everything." Skye rushes over to me and I laugh, shaking my head and heading to my room.

Skye and Aubrey follow suit when I plop down onto my bed.

"It was perfect." I sigh, blissfully. "He took me to see 'Little Shop of Horrors,' he opened doors for me, he held my hand, he told me over and over again how beautiful I looked, and *that kiss*."

"You kissed *again*?" Aubrey squeals and I motion for her to be quiet, not wanting Sunshine to hear.

"I don't know, I just, I've never felt anything like this before. I get goosebumps. Butterflies. My fucking knees went weak. I thought those were all bullshit fucking movie clichés and here I am living them."

"That's what it's *supposed* to feel like, Mi. You're supposed to feel giddy and stupid and weak in the knees. I'm just so glad you're finally letting yourself be happy." Skye hugs me.

"He asked me to be his girlfriend," I sigh, my face getting hot.

"Don't forget to buy condoms," Aubrey laughs and Skye hugs me.

"Okay listen I want to hear more, but Aubrey has a shift tomorrow morning so I really want to get back home and get some more time in with her before bed."

"Thanks for hanging out until I got back." I smile at both of them.

"You're joking, right? We were *dying* to see the two of you finally get together." Skye laughs and kisses my cheek before standing. "I love you. Have fun tomorrow. Don't do anything I wouldn't do."

I walk Skye and Aubrey to the door, offering each a hug, when I hear my phone ping with a text message from my bedroom.

> Stop thinking about me :P

The next text comes in a few seconds later.

> Actually, wait, don't.

> Goodnight, Sunshine. After that kiss, you're the only thing in my head.

> That was the goal. Goodnight, beautiful. Sweet dreams.

I lie in bed for hours and stare at the ceiling, listening to soft music and trying to force sleep to come. If I'm being honest with myself, I'm terrified. I've already checked the door multiple times to make sure it's locked, and I keep looking out my window. It's 3am and I've not gotten an ounce of sleep. Sunshine is only one floor away and I want to feel his arms wrapped around me again.

> Is it weird that I miss you even though you're literally sleeping upstairs?

He surprises me with a response just a few moments later.

> Why aren't you asleep?

> I didn't mean to wake you, I thought your phone was on silent.

> Come on, your first night sleeping alone after everything and I'm going to put my phone on silent? No way. Why are you awake?

> I haven't slept yet… I'm scared.

I hear rustling around, then the sounds of his footsteps descending the stairs. After a few moments, he knocks on my door.

"I'm sorry," I call out and he opens the door. "I shouldn't have texted you."

"No, you should always tell me if you're uncomfortable," he says. "I'm not upset. How can I help?"

"I don't know... would it be weird if I asked you to sleep in here with me?" I chew on the side of my thumb, nervous he'll confirm my suspicions.

He climbs into my bed on all fours before removing my hand from my mouth and giving me a small peck.

He lies back on the bed and opens his arms that I happily snuggle into. He's turned off my radio on the side of the bed and has barely finished with the first verse of "For Forever" from Dear Evan Hansen before I succumb to sleep.

12

After a day of cooking together, doing laundry together, and cleaning up the house, Sunshine and I retire to the couch to relax. I stare over at him, admiring his features and trying to convince myself that he's a real, live human being.

"What?" He laughs, catching me staring.

"Nothing." I shake my head, smiling. "I just, I don't know. I'm really impressed by you is all. Here you are at twenty-three with your own mortgage, co-owner of a business, and going into your senior year of college. Not only that but you're, like, actually a *good guy*. You're just... so put together, and I'm... not."

"Well, you have to remember too, a lot of it was a result of losing my mom. When she passed away, there was a decent amount of life insurance that was split between Adam, Birdie, and me. It made for a pretty good down payment plus some extra for savings."

Of course it was, duh. Why didn't I realize that? I'm sure he senses the guilt running through me by my comment because he places a hand on my knee reassuringly.

"I'm surprised you didn't put it towards school," I say. "Shit's so expensive."

"Yeah," he says. "My mom put together a college fund for me after she started the company... I'm lucky that I didn't have to take any loans out."

"You *are* lucky," I laugh. "I'll be drowning in student debt for years."

He leans back on the couch, putting an arm around my shoulders.

"Yeah, but I've got a mortgage. I think I've got you beat." He laughs.

I nod toward the blue acoustic guitar sitting off on a stand in the corner of the living room.

"I figured that was Asher or Justin's, but I assume from the two upstairs you play?"

"I dabble," he says.

"Play me something," I say and hand him the guitar.

I lie on the couch and watch him as he plays around with the tuning before he starts to play "I'm Yours" by Jason Mraz. I swear this man could heal literal wounds with his voice.

"You lied. You do more than dabble!" I laugh when he finishes. "Play me more?"

"Okay come on, this *has* to be boring for you." He smiles.

"Seriously?" I give him a doubting look. "I could listen to you sing for hours."

He moves to sit on the coffee table in front of me and plays "Till There Was You" from *The Music Man*. I sit up to face him.

"Those are some pretty good song choices," I stammer as he sets his guitar down next to him.

"I had some inspiration," he says and plays with a strand of hair between his fingers. "You're so beautiful."

I roll my eyes with a smile and look off to the side.

"I'm serious," he says. "I know you don't think so, but you are. I bet your biggest insecurity is probably one of the most beautiful things about you."

I look down and he pats my leg.

"Okay, I'll tell you my biggest insecurity and then you tell me yours," he says. "We're supposed to get vulnerable and shit with each other, right?"

"The *biggest* insecurity?" I ask.

"The biggest," he says. "You trust me?"

"Okay fine. You first."

"My hair." He sighs. "I've hated my hair for a long time. It used to be, like, wavy which looked okay but then it kinked up and became straight up curly. You can imagine the comments I've received being a guy with curly hair and an interest in musical theater…"

"Oh, sincerely fuck those people. I *love* your hair. It's one of the first things I noticed about you," I say, and run my fingers through his hair.

"Thank you. What's yours?" He asks.

I look down, nervous.

"My, uh, my thighs and hips," I stammer, closing one eye as if to brace for impact.

"Your thighs and your hips?" He asks slowly, his eyebrows raised and I nod.

"I mean, it's no secret that I could gain to lose a few pounds. James tried to help me with it a lot, but I just can't seem to get it under control I guess. He'd comment on what I ate, telling me things were going to go straight to my thighs…and he's not wrong, they're just, like, huge."

I shrug and watch as his back teeth clench down, making his jaw more pronounced.

"Fuck. Him. That guy is a total douchebag. Food *fuels* you and your body is hot as hell." He places a hand on my waist, giving it a gentle squeeze. "Every. Single. Curve. Drives me crazy."

I can't handle it anymore. I reach up and pull his lips down on mine. They crash together and it's more passionate than before. Before I know it, he's on his knees in front of me and his tongue is softly caressing mine. His hand is still at my waist and his other hand is in my hair. As he moves his hand down to my hip, I slide a hand into his hair, desperate to get him closer. He squeezes my waist and slips his thumb under the hem of my shirt, caressing the skin.

Fuck he feels good. He feels *right*. My heart races, my skin on fire with every touch when my stupid brain has to butt in.

He's done this before. He's kissed other girls like this. He's probably had sex. You're in way over your head.

"You okay?" He asks, breaking the kiss, as if sensing that I was spiraling.

"Yeah, I just, I need a breather." I smile shyly.

"Water?" He smiles.

"That would be great," I say and bring my hand to my mouth. My lips are slightly sore and I can still taste him.

"You wanna talk about it?" He asks when he returns from the kitchen, handing me a water bottle.

"About what?" I ask.

"Come on, I can tell something is bothering you. You can talk to me. That's how we figure this out." He gestures between us.

"I don't know... I don't have a lot of experience. Or, any, really. It seems so stupid, but I feel like I don't know what I'm doing and I don't want to do something wrong." I frown.

"Okay wait, it's not stupid, you feel how you feel. You've been through some tough shit, Mia. I'm here, at your pace, following your lead. If that means we stop doing something because you're uncomfortable, then we stop. I'm not going anywhere unless you tell me to. Whether we're making out, watching some corny rom coms, or just talking, I'm here. I'm not looking for some quick lay or anything," he says.

After taking a swig of my water, I wrap my arms around his neck in a hug and almost instantly feel his head rest on top of mine.

The moment is interrupted by my phone chirping with an incoming text message and I groan in annoyance as I pull it out of my pocket.

Mia. Your brother is upset that he hasn't seen you since our fight. Come over for dinner tonight. 5pm. Don't be late.

Figures there's no apology from my mom, just demands. I let out an- other frustrated groan and bury my head back into Sunshine's chest.

"Everything okay?" He asks, running his fingers through my hair.

"It's my mom. She wants me to come over for dinner tonight."

"So just tell her no if you don't want to go." He shrugs.

"I can't." I sigh. "Frankie's upset, and mom and I are going to have to talk sooner or later."

"Do you want me to go with you?"

The image of Sunshine meeting my mom is laughable. Even before I left Duke, every family dinner we've had since Mark, her most recent husband, left her has been met with snide comments, harsh looks, and awkward silences. Even *Skye* won't go to my mom's house anymore, despite my begging. Not to mention, Frankie has never done well with guys. His dad passed away at an early age, and he's never liked anyone mom's been with since. Not that I can blame him, she tends to jump from shitty guy to shitty guy. Frankie *especially* hated James. I can't watch him hate Sunshine too. This is something that's just *mine.* I won't let them ruin it.

"I couldn't do that to you." I laugh.

"How about this? I will go with you to your mom's house tonight, and in exchange you come with me to my sister's softball tournament tomorrow. I promised Birdie I'd go and pretty much my whole family will be there. They all want to meet you."

"You've told them about me?" I ask, surprised.

"Well obviously I didn't say we were dating, but yeah. Of course I did."

That damn giddy feeling has returned. He has to have said good things for them to want to meet me, right? I take a deep breath and steel myself. I can't care what my mother thinks anymore. Not about my career choices, not about my clothing, and certainly not about this relationship.

"Deal," I say and kiss his cheek before moving to my room to get ready for the dinner from hell.

Hopefully Mom will be too distracted with Sunshine's presence that she won't drill me more about James.

13

He takes over my car speakers while I drive and plays songs from musical after musical. From Moulin Rouge to Chicago to Rent, I love it. I love listening to him sing and just having fun singing with him with the radio at full blast. Something about it feels so carefree and makes me feel as if there is nothing to stress about... until we enter my neighborhood, that is. I quickly turn the volume down as we approach my block. No need to start the night off with "you listen to that shit too loudly."

"Okay." I take a breath and turn my body to Sunshine after I park in front of the house. "Remember, my mom is not the nicest and she's probably not going to like you because she doesn't like anybody. Don't take anything she says seriously."

"I'm not worried about it." He laughs. "Parents love me. Don't stress."

"I need you to understand that is literally impossible here."

I stare at the house and bite down on the cuticle surrounding my fore-finger. Sunshine lifts his hand to my face and removes my finger from my mouth, turning my focus to him and his touch. I have to force myself not to look at where our hands are connecting.

"Come on Mia, you've been doing really well, don't start this again," He rubs his thumb along my finger.

"She's probably going to have something to say about your major," I warn him.

"Believe me, I've heard it all before."

"She's probably going to mock your name."

"I've literally had this name my whole life. I'm used to it." He laughs.

"She's not a nice person," I say.

"Mia, it'll be okay." He takes my hand, giving it a quick kiss. "Stop worrying about me."

"I'm just trying to make sure you're ready," I say. "Frankie is a little... apprehensive around guys. Especially guys I bring home. He never liked James."

"I'm pretty good with kids." He smiles.

"Oh, this is a horrible idea. You are far too optimistic for this." I say as Sunshine opens my car door.

When we start heading to the door, Frankie swings it open.

"Hey Mia!"

He pulls me into a hug and eyes Sunshine skeptically.

"Hey! This is my friend Sunshine."

"What an interesting name." Mom observes as she appears behind Frankie. "You didn't tell me you were bringing a guest. Come in and sit down. Dinner will be ready in ten minutes."

She disappears back into the kitchen and I take a seat at the dining table with Sunshine and Frankie both taking a seat on either side of me.

"I missed you kid." I smile over at Frankie, giving his hair a small shake.

"I miss you too, Mia! You have to see how many new baseball cards I have in my collection now! I'll go get them." He runs off to his room.

Sunshine smiles over at me, while Mom walks in with a serving dish and sets it on the table.

"Of course she didn't miss her own mother," she scoffs. "Figures. So Sunshine, how do you know Mia?"

"Well, we met at a party on campus the first weekend she was here and we've kind of just been inseparable ever since. She's my best friend."

I can't help the smile that takes over my face and blush at the words. His best friend? Man, I like him way more than I should. Mom looks from me and over to Sunshine, a smug look on her face. It doesn't take me long to realize she's figured us out.

"*Oh*," she says. "I didn't realize you had gone off and gotten a new boyfriend. I thought James came by?"

"Yeah," I say. "He did, Mom. And he was super rude."

"Well honey, you broke his heart. You can't expect him to be *nice*," Mom says. "And quite frankly, I still don't understand *why*."

"Let's not get into that now, Mom. It's over." I warn.

Frankie returns to the dining room, enthusiastically flipping through his baseball card collection and showing me all of the athletes I've never heard of.

"Oh hey! You've got a Frank Robinson card!" Sunshine points to a card, smiling.

"Wait, you like baseball?" Frankie's eyes light up and looks over at Sunshine enthusiastically as he nods. "My dad named me after him!"

I couldn't be less interested in their topic of conversation, but watching the two of them interact makes my heart melt, even if they have to lean over me to do so.

"So." Mom interrupts them and clears her throat. "Sunshine, dear, tell me. What are you majoring in?"

"Musical theater." He's shaking his leg up and down rapidly under the table and I rest my hand on his thigh to help any nervousness that he may be feeling.

Mom is quiet for a minute, the sound of forks scraping against plates echoing throughout the room, before leaning in and whispering "James is going to be a *doctor*, Mia."

"Mom, you're being rude," I say.

"I apologize, Sunshine, I am not trying to be rude. You can understand that I want someone that can provide a good life for my daughter, can't you? I mean, where is the *money* in musical theater?"

"I think I do pretty well for myself," Sunshine says with a smile.

"Yeah, he owns a house," I say.

"Oh half of America owns a house." She waves it off as she takes a bite of her food.

I take a deep breath squeezing my thumb and forefinger over the bridge of my nose before turning to Frankie.

"Do you want to come into town with me and hang out for a bit?" I ask.

"You're leaving already? You've hardly even touched your food." Mom asks, surprise turning quickly into anger. "Well, Frankie isn't going with you. If you want to see him, you can 'hang out' here."

She slams her fork down on her plate before picking it up and walking out of the room.

"Sunshine brought you something," I say to Frankie and hand him a bag with some of his favorite candy from the gas station we stopped at on the way over.

His eyes light up when he looks inside but then he frowns.

"It's too much sugar," he says. "Mom says if I eat a lot of sugar I'll get diabetes."

"Yeah, but you're a kid," I say, nudging his arm with my elbow. "You're allowed to have a *little* sugar."

"Thank you," Frankie says to Sunshine and then turns to me. "How do you like your new school?"

"It's good!" I say. "I switched my major over to education and—"

"Mom told me. She said there's no money in it," Frankie says.

"That's not true, Frankie. Sure, it doesn't make as much as a *doctor*," I mock Mom, "But I'll be just fine."

"Oh... sorry," he says.

"Don't be. You have any fun plans this summer?" I ask.

"Just hanging out here, mostly studying," he says.

"It's summer! You should be outside playing. There's a pool at Sunshine's house if you want to come over sometime." I smile at him.

"Mom says if I spend too much time outside, I'll get skin cancer," Frankie says.

"Well, not if you wear sunscreen," I tease.

What the fuck is she doing to this kid?

"Why don't you show Sunshine the rest of your baseball collection? I'm going to go chat with Mom for a bit," I say and muss his hair before marching into the kitchen where Mom is washing dishes.

"What are you doing to that kid, Mom?" I whisper.

"Who? Frankie? I don't tell him anything that isn't true," she says.

"I swear." I seethe, shaking my head in disbelief. "If I could take him from you, I would. You have a perfectly good kid that you're turning into... *you.*"

"And what's so *wrong* with me?" She scoffs.

"Everything! Everything is wrong with you!" I whisper-yell, "You think you can control everything! How we feel, who we love, what we want to do with our life. He's a *kid*, Mom. He needs to be a *kid.*"

"I only ever did what was best for you both!" She yells back.

"And look where that's gotten me, Mom! Please don't make the same mistake with Frankie that you did with me. I am *all sorts* of fucked up, partly because of you."

She rolls her eyes and scoffs, throwing the sponge in the sink full of water, making no attempts to keep herself quiet.

"You would've been fine if you just stuck with the plan! James is a fine young man and at least *he* has a future going for him! What kind of name is *Sunshine* anyways? And who the hell majors in *musical theater*? You think I'm some heartless bitch, fine! But I care about what happens to you!"

"Mom! You can't just talk about people like that. Sunshine is literally the best person I've ever met and you've written him off already after speaking to him for a total of, what? Two minutes?"

"I don't need to talk to him more to know that he has no future!" She yells.

"You are never going to change..." I say, shaking my head and walking towards the dining room again.

Sunshine is sitting with Frankie, engrossed in a conversation about baseball and what teams are good this year. He looks up and gives me a small smile.

"I'm going to just go take a minute, okay?" I address Frankie and he waves me off, showing Sunshine another one of his cards.

I head out the front door and sit on the porch, desperately needing to put some space between my mom and me. I can't comprehend how a mom can be so... cruel? Overprotective? Controlling? I don't even know the right word for it. All I know is I need to talk some sense into her or Frankie will end up with the same problems I have. I put my head in my hands and take deep breaths, grateful to Sunshine for staying inside with Frankie. One thing is for sure— if I don't see some kind of change in her, I will no longer have a relationship with my mom.

When I walk back inside, Mom is sitting quietly in the living room with Frankie and Sunshine, reading her book.

"I want to take Frankie to Sunshine's house... our house... to swim at some point this summer," I say.

"*Your* house?" She asks.

"Yeah. Sunshine and I moved in together. You can either support me in it or not, I don't really care anymore." I shrug.

"Well I don't know that I trust you with Frankie," she says, crossing her arms, her eyebrows raised.

"Seriously? When Mark left I was all you had to help with him. You sure trusted me then," I say.

She stares at me and this time I stare right back.

"Fine." She concedes. "Just let me know when."

"What about next weekend?" I ask.

"Sure," she says. "You can come pick Frankie up at one on Saturday. Bring him home by six."

I nod and offer Frankie a soft hug and a kiss to the top of his head. To my surprise, Frankie also hugs Sunshine. At least one of them approves of my choices. Sunshine takes my hand as we start down the path to my car, rubbing his thumb along the back of my hand.

"I am so sorry," Sunshine says when we get in the car.

"You? *I'm* sorry. She's such a miserable bitch she can't be happy when anyone does something they might actually enjoy... How much did you hear?" I ask.

"All of it," he sighs "your mom isn't exactly quiet."

"You do have a future," I say. "She's dumb and we hate her. Just ignore her, I do."

He laughs and kisses my cheek.

"It takes a bit more than that to hurt my feelings... Are you okay?"

"Hopefully things go better with your family tomorrow," I let out a small laugh.

~

Sunshine woke early this morning in my bed after yet another night of being unable to fall asleep on my own. I groaned when his alarm went off, which prompted him to kiss my cheek and leave a trail of kisses all the way down to my bare shoulder, moving my tank top strap over to the side as he did. I took him up on an offer to sleep in and meet him at the field, but I can't say I'm not regretting it now. I sit on the bleachers by the field and bite my thumb, scanning the crowd for Sunshine but not finding him.

Checking the fence, I know I'm at the right field and I haven't gotten any text messages. Maybe he decided he didn't want me to meet his family yet after all. Maybe the game got cancelled. I try to calm the annoying ass doubt in my head with a deep breath and check my phone. Fifteen minutes before game time. I'm in the process of pulling up a new text to Sunshine when I finally feel his arms wrap around me from behind and his lips press firmly against my cheek. When I turn to face him with a smile, he signs and speaks simultaneously.

"Hey, sorry I had to pee and Birdie forgot her water so I bought her one. This is Birdie," he says signing her name sign.

She signs so fast it's hard to keep up with what she's saying, but I can't help but notice how pretty she is. She has the same black hair as Sunshine, but hers is more wavy and probably lays down to the middle of her back at least when it's not up in a ponytail. Her eyes are more hazel than his, but they have the same shimmery blue shine around the edges. I'll have to remember to ask him to see a picture of his mom because she must've been beautiful to produce such gorgeous children.

"Slow down," Sunshine signs, letting out a small laugh. "She's still learning."

"Sorry. Nice to meet you," Birdie signs and smiles.

I got an A in ASL last semester, but I am nowhere near fluent, so I'm grateful when Sunshine interprets for me.

"It's about time my brother finds a pretty girl," she signs.

"Hey!" Sunshine says, feigning offense and musses her hair.

She laughs and I can't help but smile. Their relationship is adorable.

"Thank you," I sign.

Birdie talks about softball and how she's excited that I'm here. She says that Sunshine talks about me every time she sees him and I watch a red hue creep up to his cheeks. He watches as she signs and suddenly stops interpreting. They go into a conversation and I watch, but they're signing too fast for me to keep up. I catch only a few words from Birdie- girlfriend, dating, and love. Wait, what?

"I'm lost," I sign and smile sheepishly.

"Oh, she was just saying she loves your shoes," he signs as he talks. Birdie looks down at my shoes and smiles.

"They *are* cute." She smiles, intentionally signing slower as she points at Sunshine. "But you're a liar."

Birdie walks off into the dugout and I look at Sunshine confused.

"She's crazy." He laughs and I eye him suspiciously. He smiles sheepishly and kisses my cheek again.

As the team warms up on the field, Sunshine waves over to a group of four people, who light up when they see him. Given their similar tanned skin and dark hair, it must be his family. I take a deep, steadying breath. I knew James' family before we ever even started dating, so I've never had to meet my boyfriend's family before. It feels so damned intimidating that I can't keep from biting the skin around my nails. Sure enough, Sunshine removes my hand from my mouth and holds it, giving it a small reassuring squeeze.

Sunshine gestures to a beautiful, tall, and very pregnant woman with curly brown hair and bright eyes. I swear if I didn't know any better, I'd think this was Sunshine's mom. He introduces her as his Aunt Julie, his mom's younger sister. Following her is a man, probably about the same height as her if not maybe a few inches shorter with shaggy blonde hair and dark eyes. I learn that this is Travis, Julie's fiancé. Sunshine then moves to an older woman in a walker and takes her bag from her as she makes her way over to me.

"Is this Mia?" She smiles at me and then looks up at Sunshine.

"Yeah, Grams, this is Mia... my girlfriend." Sunshine says, smiling proudly as he wraps his arm around my waist.

"I knew it," Julie says, smiling and wraps her arms around me in a hug, her swollen belly getting in the way.

"Knew what?" A man asks, coming up behind Sunshine's grandmother, giving Sunshine a quick hug. He holds his hand out to shake mine and introduces himself as Adam, Birdie's dad and Sunshine's stepdad.

"Sunshine here has a girlfriend," Julie says, teasingly.

"We should watch the game, yeah?" Sunshine laughs, changing the subject.

Julie and Sunshine's grandmother, whose name I've learned is Sherri, have been asking me a variety of questions, with Birdie throwing in a few of her own when she has a break between games, ranging from my major to my religion. Or rather, lack thereof. I had felt really bad for Sunshine when he went through a similar thing last night with my mom, but his family is so much nicer about it. Travis has been quiet the majority of the time, and Adam is keeping score close to the dugout.

Birdie is a natural at softball. When her team wins the tournament, I can see the pride in Sunshine's face as he cheers loudly. Sunshine offers me a quick kiss before he heads to the concession stand to grab some food. I opt to sit with Birdie and the rest of his family are wrapped up in conversation.

"He really likes you," she signs slowly.

"I really like him, too," I sign.

"I don't think I've ever seen him so happy. He's my best friend."

She laughs when she has to sign some words more than once. Fuck I need to learn ASL faster.

"He loves you. I hope that we can be friends too." I smile at her and she hugs me.

"I knew you'd love her," Sunshine signs after tapping her on the shoulder and handing her a hot dog. He hands one to me and then passes more out to the rest of his family members.

Birdie smiles and gives Sunshine a mischievous look. He gives her a small warning look and they both laugh, clearly reveling in some inside joke.. I'm lost but I smile anyways.

"I'm riding home with Sunshine!" She signs to her dad as she hops in the backseat of his car. "You don't mind driving me home, right?"

"I'll see you back at the house," I say to Sunshine. I walk to Birdie to hug her goodbye and she pulls back after a moment.

"Please don't hurt him," she signs after a few minutes, as Sunshine is caught up in conversation with Adam about the business.

"I don't plan on it," I sign back slowly.

"When he and Natalie broke up, he was heartbroken for months. I can't see him like that again." She signs.

I offer her a soft smile, unsure how to respond. Who the hell is Natalie? Sunshine walks over to me from around the car and gives me a lingering kiss.

I can't help but let doubt creep in while I drive back to the house.

Natalie. Not a name I've heard before. Of course, I knew he had girl-friends in the past, but he's never mentioned any of them. Certainly not one that broke his heart.

When I pull up to the house, I immediately head for the bathroom to clean the sweat of the day off of me. When I open the linen closet to grab a towel, I notice female toiletries on the top shelf. It's not the same brands I use... did they belong to Natalie? I shake away the thought and grab a towel and turn the water on to hot.

Sunshine is cooking dinner after I get out of the shower and I stand next to the counter. I watch as he looks me over in my short pajama shorts and tank top, his gaze heavy.

"Hi," he smiles.

"Hey," I smile back. He's listening to punk music and chopping carrots. "I've got to ask you something before I drive myself crazy."

"What's up?" He asks.

"Before I moved in, did you have girls here a lot or something?" I ask.

"Uhm, no? Why do you ask?"

"No... girlfriends or anything?"

"I haven't dated anyone since I bought the house... why?"

I stay quiet for a moment. I know it's technically my bathroom now, but it still felt like snooping. We *just* started dating and no one likes a girl who's jealous...

"You can tell me anything, you know," he prompts.

"There were some, like, feminine products in my bathroom closet... and I-"

He cuts me off by laughing quietly and I immediately feel embarrassed. Of course he thinks it's silly that I'm snooping in my own bathroom. Of course he thinks my finding feminine products is funny.

"Fucking Birdie," he laughs again. "She's *always* trying to claim that bedroom as hers. I swear she leaves more and more shit behind every time she comes over."

A wave of relaxation goes through me. Birdie. Duh. Of course he has stuff for his sister in the house.

"I have another question... who was Natalie?"

"Ahh, the dreaded exes talk." He laughs.

"I figure it's only fair since you know, like, literally everything about my only relationship." I say.

"I guarantee there is far more to unpack there, but I suppose you're right," He sighs. "It was just shy of a year and a half."

"That's it? What's your longest relationship?" I ask.

"Just shy of a year and a half," he laughs. "She was my only real relationship."

"Really? I figured you would have had plenty of girls." I say.

"Oh, I did…" he winces at the memory. "Before Natalie I had quite the… hookup phase. I'm not proud of it. I was a different person then and hanging out with the wrong people."

"Oh," I say and he stops chopping.

"I'm not that person anymore."

"No no I know you're not. I'm just processing. Honestly, it makes you more human." I laugh.

"More human?" He laughs and looks at me as if I'm being ridiculous.

"Yeah, I mean you're kind of perfect." I say.

"Believe me, I am *definitely* not without my flaws." He kisses me softly. "But I like that you think I'm perfect."

"Why did things with Natalie end?" I ask.

"Ultimately? She cheated on me. Like, multiple times with multiple different guys."

I look at him with sympathy. Who could cheat on a guy like Sunshine? Literal perfection in human form, even if he doesn't think so.

"But also, I didn't give her the attention she needed. We both made mistakes. You don't need to feel bad for me. Two years of being single and a year of therapy and I'm good."

"Why didn't you give her the attention she needed?" I ask.

"Well, around the one year mark is when my mom first got diagnosed. It was supposed to be a really 'easy' cancer, if you can ever call cancer easy. It was stage one, non-aggressive. We assumed that she would do some treatments and we'd be done with it. She just kept getting worse though— the cancer kept progressing and treatments made her really sick. It was just the three of us most of the time because Josh was working so much to keep the business going and if I wasn't driving her to treatments so Birdie could get time with her dad, I was taking care of Birdie. Or taking care of Mom. Or helping with the business. And when I did have some time to myself, I just wanted to be by myself. I didn't *want* to see Natalie. Sure, I'd see her every once in a while to maintain the relationship but even when I saw her I wasn't *there*, you know?" He shrugs.

"Wait, so let me get this straight," I say, sitting up, "*Your* mom gets diagnosed with *cancer* and you're doing everything you can to help your family so that gives her the right to *cheat* on you? Multiple times?"

"I don't know, I guess I'm just saying I get that I didn't give her what she needed."

"She didn't give you what you needed!" I exclaim. "She was being *selfish*! Why not, I don't know, offer to take your mom to her treatments for you. Or offer to come by while you're helping out with your sister?"

"I guess her neighbor had died of lung cancer like the year prior so she said she couldn't handle being around it."

"Her neighbor?! That was your *mom*!" I fume and he laughs. "Why are you laughing? This is horrible!"

"I just like this side of you, it's cute." He smiles. "All protective and whatnot. Look, it's in the past. It was what it was."

"Did you love her?" I ask.

"I did," he says, nodding.

"Oh..." I say. The jealousy stings.

"But she's not part of my life anymore. And there are *definitely* no leftover feelings there. Nothing to worry about," he smiles.

"I wish you didn't have to go through all that." I cuddle up next to him again.

"You know what I wish?" He asks and I look up at him. "I wish you had realized like three years ago what an absolute tool your ex was. That way I could have found you sooner. My mom would have *loved* you."

I wrap my arms around his waist and watch as he continues to chop vegetables. He leans over and kisses the top of my head.

"So I have a question too," he says.

"What?" I laugh.

"What's your stance on intimacy?" he asks and I nearly choke out a laugh. "Sorry, are you uncomfortable?"

"No, not uncomfortable per se. That was just kind of out of nowhere. I also don't usually talk about this kind of stuff out loud. Sex wasn't really allowed to be a topic of conversation growing up. Mom just expected abstinence. I've done... some stuff, but not a lot."

"I'm sorry," he says "it definitely doesn't have to be a taboo subject around me. I always want to know what you're thinking and I want to make sure I know where you stand so I don't cross any boundaries."

"I don't know," I shrug, "I guess I just need to go with what feels right. Like, I know I really love kissing you."

"Well that's good, because I'm a pretty big fan of that too." He responds with a devilish smile.

"Can I help at all?" I ask, gesturing to the cutting board.

"Yes actually," he says, putting his knife down.

He picks me up by my legs and I think for a moment that he's going to wrap my legs around his waist when he puts me down on the countertop. He stands between my legs and runs a hand through the underside of my hair.

"You can stop being so damn distracting," he smiles and kisses me deeply.

"I was just standing here," I laugh.

"Exactly," he smiles and kisses me again, pulling me closer to him. My breath leaves me and my stomach tightens as the simmering vegetables begin to sizzle. "I should get back to cooking before I burn the house down."

Such a fucking tease he is. I watch as he continues to sauté onions before adding the carrots.

"What about the other important stuff— kids, and marriage and stuff? Is that something you'd want?" I ask.

Why? Why would I allow those words to come out of my mouth? I don't even know where *I* stand on these things for sure. My heart races with panic at the word marriage that I hardly hear his response. He gives me a confused look and seems to think about it a moment before smiling at me.

"Yeah, someday."

Fuck, fuck, fuck.

"I think it's probably important that you know... I don't know if I ever want to get married..." I trail. "I already had one engagement that didn't work out, I don't really want to add a failed marriage on top of it."

"Wait, really?" He asks, surprised.

"Yeah, I don't know. I can't tell if it's something I ever wanted or if it was just another thing my mom expected of me. I think if you're with the right person then it shouldn't matter. I mean, it's just a piece of paper." I shrug.

"I disagree. It's the ultimate commitment. Telling the person you love that you'd rather be dead than be without them? It's kind of poetic."

"I just don't see it that way. I think you can tell them with words without spending thousands of dollars on a wedding," I say and there's a sense of awkwardness in the air.

"I get that," He nods, "But one can get married without the fancy, several thousand dollar wedding."

"Yeah, I guess. I don't know... I just never saw the point in it. I feel like all it achieves is making it expensive to fall out of love with someone," I shrug.

"Do you think people fall out of love that easily?" He asks.

"Well no, I don't think it's *easy* necessarily. But it happens," I shrug, "It happened to my parents."

"I don't think I've ever heard you talk about your dad."

"He hasn't been around for a long time," I nod. "He doesn't deserve my attention."

He finishes up cooking and it smells amazing.

"What about kids?" He asks, plating the food.

"I... don't know that I want kids either," I hesitate telling him.

"Can I ask why?" He asks.

"I don't know... all I ever hear from parents is how they don't feel like themselves anymore and how expensive they are... it also just seems like a *lot* of responsibility to try and not fuck up another human being..."

He nods as he helps me down from the counter and brings my plate to the table, me following close behind him.

I've ruined everything. Where can we really go if we want different things?

"Do you want a pop?" He asks before sitting my plate in front of me.

"No thank you," I say quietly, "I'll stick to water."

He sits next to me and puts a hand on my thigh before he starts eating.

The silence is overwhelming as we both eat, the only sound being the silverware hitting the plates. I feel like my heart is breaking. I *finally* gave in to Sunshine only to realize we aren't exactly compatible. Where the hell are we supposed to go from here?

"I'm sorry," I say after several silent moments.

"For what?" He asks.

"Not wanting the same things you want... making things awkward..." I trail.

"It's just going to be something we'll have to navigate together," he shrugs and keeps eating.

"How?" I ask with tears in my eyes, "How can we? Our futures look so different."

He turns in his seat to face me.

"Because we can get through anything," he wipes my tears.

"You deserve to have everything you want," I say, shaking my head.

"I *want* you. We'll figure the rest out later." He moves a piece of hair behind my ear.

I kiss him and he cradles my face, kissing me back. Tears are still falling and he wipes them away with his thumbs. I don't want this to end. I don't want to lose him. I have to show him. I make a move to get closer to him and stand, still kissing him.

"Where are you going?" He asks between kisses and I straddle his lap.

He looks up at me and smiles. I move one of his hands to my hip and kiss him again, my hand gripping at his curls. I need him to feel just how badly I want him. I need to convince him to stay. I feel him grow hard beneath me and heat rises beneath my cheeks. My hips move against him almost involuntarily causing his breath to hitch and I kiss his neck. One of his hands is gripping lightly at the back of my hair and the other is firmly planted at my waist. I move my hands down his chest and to the waistband of his pants. I have to do this.

"Hey, hey, wait," he whispers.

"What?" I ask and he wipes a few tears away.

I didn't even realize they were falling faster.

"Are you ok? We don't have to do anything you're not comfortable with. I'm happy just to spend time with you." He rubs his thumb against my cheek and I absolutely lose it, becoming a sobbing mess.

What the fuck is even happening right now? I cry for several moments as Sunshine continues to wipe the tears away, making soothing noises.

"Stop," I say, frustrated and move away from his hand.

"Stop what?" He asks. "Comforting you?"

"No," I snap. "Looking at me like that. Like I'm a wounded animal."

"What?" He asks, concerned and confused.

Birdie's face appears in my mind as she asks me not to hurt him. We may have been inevitable, but so is our demise, so I might as well save us both some hurt. There's no way for us to stay together and both get what we want, and I care about him too much to let him settle. I take a deep breath. No matter how much I want him, I have to let him go. It's better to hurt him a little now and save him time than let it continue and hurt him way more when we eventually realize that we're just too different. He'll find someone better. Someone prettier, someone more successful, someone who wants all of the things he wants. This is the right choice. I fight back the tears that threaten to spill.

"You act like I'm this broken person," I say, trying my hardest to convince both of us that I'm angry. "Like I need saving. Like you're my knight in shining fucking armor."

Tears spill from my eyes, betraying me. This is pathetic.

"I'm not broken, Sunshine. I don't need saving and I don't need your pity. Before I met you I was a pretty strong person, but you're making me weak... I don't think I can do this after all."

"Come on, Mia, don't do that," he holds my face. "Please don't push me away."

He looks so sad as he holds my gaze and I can hardly handle it. I sob and try to stop myself. This is *not* helping my case. He holds me and gently rocks me. I start to push away from him but my body stays as if against my will. As if he has this magnetic force that I can't break.

"You're not broken. You're one of the strongest people I've ever met. I'm so sorry if I made you feel anything less. The way I see it, you've spent the majority of your life taking care of yourself *and* your brother. That's not *normal*, Mia. I want to take care of you and I just want you to be happy. You're happy with me, right? We can figure it all out, I promise. Don't give up on us when we've only barely started."

"I can't be what you need," I sob.

"But you already are. If you don't want to get married, I don't need it. If you don't want kids, that's fine. I'm here for whatever. I want you in my life. The rest is flexible," he pleads.

Why does he know the exact right things to say? He doesn't want me to settle... but isn't that what he's doing? Settling?

"I need to go," I say, standing up, "I can't handle this right now. I'm going to go stay with Skye tonight."

"Wait, are we okay?" He pleads, grabbing my hand.

"We'll talk tomorrow," I sigh.

I walk to my car, sobbing. I wait until I calm down before I start driving and hit the button to call Skye on my way. Hopefully I won't be putting them out too much by staying on their couch.

14

When I get to their apartment, I avoid Skye's embrace and head straight for the bathroom. The fear and heartache hits me like a ton of bricks as I sob and empty the contents of my stomach. The night went from perfect to horrible in the matter of minutes and I'm the one to blame. For once, Skye doesn't push and just offers a hug when I emerge from the bathroom while Aubrey makes up the couch with a blanket and pillow. I thank each of them before they retire to their bedroom.

I lay on the couch and stare at the ceiling, both fear and devastation pulling at my heartstrings. I want more than anything to sleep and just not wake up, but sleep won't come no matter how much I try. Around four am my phone chirps on the floor and I rush to silence it when I see there is a text from Sunshine.

> Are you awake?

> Yes. Why are you?

> I don't like how we left things. And I don't know where we stand. So I couldn't sleep.

> I'll come back around 8 or so and we'll talk.

I power my phone off and continue to stare at the ceiling. I'm not ready to talk to him. Not being with Sunshine is the right thing to do, and I know he's going to try to do everything he can to convince me it's not. Everyone will. And fuck it, maybe they're right. Maybe leaving him isn't the right thing to do... I don't even know anymore. I just know that he deserves so much better than me.

At two minutes to eight, I knock on Sunshine's front door. I have a key, but it feels too weird to use it right now. It doesn't feel like it belongs to me. I haven't seen Sunshine look so rough. There are dark circles under his eyes and he's wearing a somber look. I walk into the house and sit in my book nook, Sunshine following me.

"Can I hug you?" he asks.

I offer him a small hug and stare out the window, watching a bird in the giant tree out front give food to her babies. It's silent for several moments as I try to think of what to say to him. As I wrestle with myself over what the right decision is.

"I didn't sleep at all last night," I sigh. "I was thinking a lot about the past year and how the entire trajectory of my life changed. I don't know that I've told you but I got an RA job when I left James. Lived on my own in the dorms, which I was surprisingly okay with. But I still had to see him everyday in class. He looked completely broken and I *know* I gave him some of the looks I see from you. I was on a career path that was never my choice, with a mom that expected perfection and compliance twenty four seven, a best friend who was pissed at me and rightfully so, and at a school full of stuck-up people who wanted to prove they were better than you every two seconds. I was completely alone... I, uh, I called Skye because I wanted to apologize... I needed her to understand why I couldn't do it anymore."

"Do what?" He asks, patiently wiping tears away from my cheeks.

"Any of it. The expectations, the pressure... just life," I admit. "And then in typical Skye fashion she whipped my ass into shape and talked me down... convinced me to take control of my life and what I wanted..."

I stay focused on the bird's nest outside, doing everything I can to not look at him.

"She flew into Raleigh the next morning, helped get my shit situated there, packed all my stuff into a moving van, and drove behind me all the way here... she quite literally saved my life. And I can never repay her. What I can do is make sure I never get to that place again..." I take a deep breath. "This doesn't even have anything to do with you. I think I need to see someone, Sunshine. With everything that's happened, I'm *not* okay. I probably should have realized it sooner, but I'm just not."

"Did you have a plan?" he asks.

"I did," I confirm.

"Did you see anyone? Did you get help?" He asks.

"No, after I moved here I was fine... until the break in. I need to figure my shit out, and I don't want to drag you down while I do..."

He's silent for a long moment and I can feel him slightly moving next to me but I remain fixated on the tree, the mother bird having left her babies on their own in the nest.

"I disagree," he says, "I can be here *while* you figure out what's going on. If you want to go to counseling, I support you. You want to go get a tattoo? Sure why the hell not. If you want to scream into a pillow or beat the shit out of some punching bags, I say what time and where? You don't have to go through this alone."

"You deserve a girl who can be present with you and focused on *you*, not herself." I say, tears still rolling down the side of my face.

"No fuck that!" He exclaims, his voice wavering a bit. It takes everything I have not to look at him. But I can't. I know if I do I'll give in. "Fuck that, Mia, because I'm not perfect, either. I know you like to look at me like I am, but I'm not. All I'm asking is to be here with you. To help you. To grow *with* you."

"Sunshine..." I start.

"Are you happy with me?" He asks, cutting me off.

"You know I am," I try to hide the crying in my voice.

"Then just *be* happy with me," he pleads.

"It's not right," I whisper.

"Not right for who? Because *this* sure as hell isn't right for me," he says.

"You need to find someone who can give you what you need," I say.

"*You* are what I need," he says.

I feel him shift next to me and then he's hovering over me, his eyes piercing into my soul.

"I'm falling in love with you, Mia," he says, "That's not something I say lightly. It may be too soon, and I'm not expecting you to say anything in return but I am falling for you, hard and fast. No one else can give me what I need because no one else is you. I am begging you, please don't do this."

I stare at him. Love? It's way too soon. That can't be what this is.

"You know that if I thought for one second you actually wanted this I would let you go, but I can see in your eyes that you don't," he says. "Tell me I'm wrong."

"Of course I don't. But I don't want to hurt you. I *can't* hurt you."

"Why don't you sleep on it? Neither one of us slept last night, we're both exhausted. This is no state to be making decisions in. Let's take a nap. The counseling center will be open when we wake up and then you can set up an appointment. Can I please hold you, and sleep next to you?" He asks and I hesitate but nod. He takes my hand and leads me to the couch, opening his arms for me. I curl into him and fall asleep nearly immediately.

When I wake I'm cuddled into him, my legs tangled up in his and both of our arms wrapped around each other. My face is inches from his. He feels like home. I can't let this go, I'm too far in. I start crying. Again.

"Hey, hey, shh," He runs his fingers through my hair, "What's wrong?"

"I'm scared," I say.

"I'm right here, no one is getting in here," he replies.

"No," I breathe, "Of this. I'm scared of hurting you. I'm scared of getting hurt."

"Right," he says, "How about this? Open communication, always. If either of us are feeling any type of way, we'll talk about it, and we'll agree that if it doesn't work out between us, we will always be friends."

He looks away from me and I pull his chin back toward me. The hurt in his eyes is almost unbearable. All of this back and forth is hurting him, too. He's too far in at this point, and getting hurt is inevitable either way. I tried and tried to put space between us, but it didn't work.

"I don't want this to end," I say.

He pulls me into a tight hug and kisses me passionately.

"I still need to get help," I say, "we can't sleep together every night."

"I disagree on that last part but hey, if I have an opportunity to be around you I want to take it."

I call the counseling center with Sunshine hugging me around the waist, his head in my lap, and lazily play with his curls. I explain the urgency of the need and since it's summer, they're able to fit me in later today. Sunshine drives me, holding my hand a little tighter as we drive, and squeezing it for reassurance every so often.

There were a lot of questionnaires I had to fill out before I found myself sitting awkwardly in the office of Melissa Travis. Everything in this room feels so sterile. I'm not quite sure where to start so I start at the beginning. From the never-ending, impossible expectations from my mom, all the way through to my current relationship with Sunshine and everything in between.

After an hour of crying, it doesn't feel any less awkward, but I feel so much lighter. When I walk outside Sunshine is singing in his car in the same spot I left him in.

"You were right," I sigh, when I get in the car. "And I hate saying that."

"About what?" he laughs.

"Not breaking up... my counselor said it sounded like we have a good relationship... she also said I needed to make sure I'm getting good sleep... would it be terrible if we just shared a bed for a little while? Just until I can work through some of this with her."

"You won't hear me complain. You can just move your stuff into my room," he says, looking from me to the road as he drives.

"We've been together for less than a week, Sunshine. It's way too soon," I say.

"Well first of all, we've hung out nearly daily for like six months. Typically? Sure. When your girlfriend had her apartment broken into and ransacked and she's now too scared to sleep alone? Nah. Besides, who pays attention to 'normal' when it comes to relationships?" he says.

I switch the car to play audio from my phone and turn on the soundtrack of *Rent*. I listen as Sunshine serenades me with *I'll Cover You* and smile, singing right along with him and trying to forget this lousy day.

15

The last week has flown by between work and playing house with Sunshine. My second counseling appointment was yesterday and I'm feeling confident about finally sleeping in my own room, especially since I've finally started decorating it to my satisfaction. I'm folding clothes on my bed when I hear a knock on the open door and look up to see Sunshine leaning against the frame, looking just as bit delicious as he has every other day.

"You don't have to knock," I laugh.

"I want to make sure you know you have your privacy," he says, smiling "Just like my other *roommates*."

He walks over to my bed and sits on the edge, helping me fold.

"I think I'm going to try to sleep in here tonight," I say.

"Whatever you want, roomie. Just know my bed is open to you," he teases.

I kiss him. Something about all of it feels so *normal*. Like we've known each other for years.

"You want to go for a swim?" he asks.

"Sure," I shrug and grab my suit from my drawer.

The face Sunshine makes when I come into the living room in my suit makes me feel *seen*. Wanted.

"Race you there," I giggle and run out the back door, Sunshine following behind me and discarding his shirt along the way.

I jump in the pool right before he's able to catch me and the water shifts as he jumps in after me.

"Where the hell did this Mia come from?" He asks when we both resurface, pushing his hair out of his face.

I turn and take in his muscled chest and six pack and can't help but bite my lower lip, because holy shit he is hot.

"I can be adventurous on occasion." I shrug.

He walks closer to me and wraps his arms around my waist.

"You are gorgeous." He says, looking me up and down. "Absolutely gorgeous."

"Me?" I say, "Have you looked in the mirror? I mean, holy muscles Batman."

He laughs and I think he's going to kiss me, but then he swims to the side of me.

"Where are you going?" I ask and he covers his eyes.

"Marco," he says and I let out a laugh before I take off under the water.

"Polo," I yell from across the pool and splash water in his direction.

He rushes in my direction, his muscles rippling as he swims.

"Marco?" He asks when he's a few feet away.

"Polo," I say quietly.

He edges closer to me and I stay completely still against the edge of the pool.

"Marco?" He asks, more curiously.

"Polo," I whisper and splash a small amount of water in his direction.

He's inches from me when he calls out again and I whisper in response until he's caging me in between his arms and his face is hovering over mine.

"Marco?" He whispers, his smile inches from my mouth.

"Polo," I whisper and he kisses me hard.

I run my fingers through his hair and kiss him back. One strong arm moves to my waist and the other wraps around to my lower back. I let one hand roam to his biceps and the other stays in his hair, moving his soft curls through my fingers. I pull him closer to me, wrapping my legs around his waist, and he kisses my neck. I bite my lip and let out a groan as his kisses become softer and sweeter. He looks at me with a smile and kisses the tip of my nose.

~

Of course, I can't fall asleep on my own. A few counseling sessions wasn't going to change that. I walk slowly and quietly up to Sunshine's room where he's sleeping peacefully, lying on his stomach. I slowly pull the covers back and slide in next to him, careful not to wake him. It was no use and I should have known better. He moves on to his side and opens his arms. I smile and cuddle into him. He falls back to sleep quickly and I briefly watch him sleep before I fall asleep myself.

Sunshine nuzzles into my hair as I wake up, and I smile. Cuddling with Sunshine is probably my favorite activity. He's so warm and comfortable. I shift against him, trying to get closer, and feel a stickiness between my legs. My eyes open in panic and I quickly shift out of his grip and stand.

"What? What? What?" He asks, mirroring my panic.

When I pull the covers back there's a small puddle of blood, as suspected.

"Oh my God," I say, completely mortified, "I am so so sorry. Watch out, let me get the sheet off and I'll clean it. God I hope it didn't go through to the bed." I start to strip the bed and Sunshine grabs my wrist.

"Babe, it's fine. It happens," he smiles at me and rubs the sleepiness out of his eyes.

"It's so gross, I'm so sorry. It's not regular and I never really know when it's going to pop up but I usually can tell better than thi-"

"Stop. I'm not worried about it. Go grab a shower and I'll clean this up. If you leave your pajamas outside the door I'll wash those too." He stands and strips the bed and the waterproof cover.

"Really?" I ask.

"Absolutely." He asks.

"It's just that James always-" I start but I'm cut off.

"I'm not James. Go on, I've got this." He kisses my forehead and I head to the bathroom. I put my pajamas and underwear outside the door as he requested.

After I finish in the shower, I crack the door open to the bedroom to make sure he's not there. Walking into the bedroom, I find that he's laid comfy clothes from my room on the bed along with some chocolate, pain killers, and pads. He really does think of everything. After walking downstairs, I find Sunshine relaxing on the couch playing a video game that he pauses when he hears me.

"I've got a movie pulled up and a heating pad here," he smiles at me and I cuddle into him. "And there's chocolate ice cream in the freezer."

"You are absolute perfection," I sigh as I make myself comfortable against him.

"Let's go to New York next weekend," Sunshine whispers against my hair as he holds me.

"That's random," I laugh, "Why New York?"

"Jason Jacobs is playing Fiyero in Wicked. I figured you might want to see it," he says.

"Oh. My. God. For real? That would be so cool to see," I say.

"So let's see it," he shrugs.

"I can't afford to go to New York and you know it," I say.

"I didn't ask if you could afford it. I can and I want to take you. Have you ever been?" he asks.

"No," I say. "I've pretty much only been to North Carolina... unless you count driving through states to get there."

"Your mom never took you on vacation?" he asks and I give him a look. He's met my mom. "Right. Well then we *have* to go. You deserve a vacation."

"I don't know..." I start.

"I'm booking our plane tickets now. Maybe we'll go to the beach after... we could make it like a week long thing and just go and-"

"Woah woah woah," I laugh, "That's way too much."

"Okay, okay. Just New York then. One weekend. For now." He sighs.

"Fine," I say, "I *guess* I'll let you take me on a romantic weekend away."

He kisses me, smiling. I wrap my arms around his neck and we kiss lazily for a while before it gets more and more intense. His hand squeezes my thigh and I move my hands to the hem of his shirt. He smiles, sits up, and pulls his shirt over his head. I pull him down on me to kiss his neck, coaxing the most delicious sound out of him. A sense of anxiety flutters in my chest and I slow, Sunshine following my cues.

"Sorry," I say.

"For what?" he asks, moving a piece of hair behind my ear.

"Honestly, I don't know. I'm so comfortable around you, but it's like every time I touch you, I get so anxious that I can't think straight."

"I'm not worried about it," he kisses the tip of my nose. "There's never any rush. Come on, let's grab showers so we can go get the kiddos for swimming."

~

Picking up Frankie is awkward as hell. Mom and I both know there's not a whole lot that we can say to one another given everything that's happened, and she's not going to apologize for not agreeing with what I want. Luckily Frankie doesn't pick up on too much of the drama as he talks on and on about some new model car he got on the way to the house. Meanwhile I'm trying to explain to him that Birdie is Deaf and offer up some signs that may be useful for him.

When we walk through the gate to the backyard, Birdie and Sunshine are already in the pool. He's splashing her when we walk up.

"Hey!" I say and wave.

"Mia!" Birdie signs and hops out of the pool.

She runs over to me and gives me a hug, soaking the front of my shirt. Sunshine laughs and I hug her back.

"Thanks for getting me wet," I sign to her, laughing.

"You're welcome," She signs back, "This is your brother?"

I nod and Sunshine hops out of the pool.

"Nice to meet you," She turns to Frankie and I interpret.

Frankie pulls a phone out and types out something that she reads. He and Birdie head over to some lounge chairs and type back and forth.

"Hi," Sunshine smiles and pulls me into a hug.

"What is with you and your family getting me wet?!" I laugh.

"I bet that's not the only place I make you wet," he whispers with a laugh and plants a soft kiss on my neck, causing the hair on my arms to stand.

"There are children present," I laugh with him.

"Go get your suit on," he says, smiling.

"Fine," I smile, "But no splashing."

I rush into the house and pick out a modest blue bikini, grateful for the tampons stocked in my bathroom. When I come back downstairs Sunshine is gathering snacks in the kitchen, but he stops when he sees me.

"Are you sure I can't talk you into some light splashing? We can play in my bedroom," he smiles and looks me up and down.

"Pervert," I jest.

He moves toward me and wraps his arms around me, his hands sliding to my ass.

"How did I get so lucky? I've got a girlfriend who is *smoking* hot, smart, generous, *and* kind. You're like perfection wrapped up in a person."

I kiss him in response.

"I'm not perfect, but I like that you think I am." I quote what he once told me.

"Oh! Do you care if I invite over the rest of the family? Aunt Julie keeps complaining about the heat with the baby," he looks down at me.

"It's your house," I shrug, "invite whoever you want."

"It's *our* house now, baby," he smiles and kisses me again.

I smile at him and nod before helping him bring the snacks outside.

We lounge by the pool while Birdie and Frankie play, often using his phone to type back and forth to each other. I feel Sunshine's eyes on me every so often and it lights up my soul. I've never had anyone look at me the way he does. Like he wants to cherish every part of me while also absolutely devouring me.

"Hello, hello!" I hear Julie call before she opens the gate to the backyard.

Sunshine jumps up from the lounge chair next to me.

"Hey Aunt Julie!" He exclaims and hugs her, "come on in."

"Mia! It's so nice to see you again." She exclaims when she sees me, and wraps an arm around me and then turns to Sunshine again. "Mom said she's coming by too?"

"Yeah, I figured she was riding with you," he says.

"You know how she is. She's probably got her new boy toy bringing her," Julie rolls her eyes.

"Come on, Henry is hardly new," Sunshine laughs, "You're just jealous your mom still has it going on and can pick up guys at bingo."

"Okay, ew." Julie shudders and Sunshine laughs again.

"Where's Travis?" Sunshine asks, taking Julie's bag from her hand.

"Oh who knows," she waves him off, clearly annoyed. "Probably golfing or something."

"Hello?" I hear an elderly voice come from by the gate and Sunshine puts Julie's bag down by another lounge chair before rushing over.

He opens the gate and Sherri walks through, using a walker this time.

"Where's Henry, Grams?" Sunshine asks.

"Oh he'll come back and get me later. He had some errands to run." She waves him off. She's unsteady on her feet.

She hugs me when she sees me and offers me a wide smile. I put my hand on her back and help her navigate the backyard while Sunshine carries her bags.

"Jeez Gram, what did you bring?" Sunshine laughs as I help Sherri take a seat at the patio.

"I can't come to my grandson's house without a gift for my grandbabies. It's poor grandma etiquette. I brought something for Mia, too," she smiles.

Birdie hops out of the pool and rushes over to Sherri, Frankie trailing behind her. I introduce her to Frankie before Birdie hugs her and heads back to the pool. I take everyone's drink requests and walk toward the house to get them.

"Sunshine Noah, I know your mother raised you better than to let a woman wait on you, hand and foot! Get in there and help her fetch those drinks!" She teases Sunshine and he smiles at her.

"Yes, Grams." he says and follows me into the house.

"Sorry," he laughs slightly, "I shouldn't have needed her to tell me to come help you."

"It's fine," I laugh and kiss his cheek. "But how did I not know your middle name?"

"Huh," he says, surprised. "I don't know, but I don't know yours either."

"It's Harper. Mia Harper." I say.

"It's beautiful," he smiles, putting his hands on my waist, "Just like you."

He kisses me, running his hands in my hair, and I'm lost in him. His hands immediately find my waist and I let out a whimper, trying to keep the inevitable anxiety that won't fuck off from taking over.

"Ahem," Julie clears her throat, "Aunt coming in."

"Sorry, Aunt Julie," Sunshine blushes.

"Nah, don't be. I get it. Just remember sometimes that leads to this." She points to her stomach and we both laugh.

The whole day is just so... normal. I couldn't say when the last time my family had any kind of cookout was, if we ever even had one, but it's a breath of fresh air. Sunshine's family is so warm and welcoming, a stark contrast to mine. Everyone laughs and teases and has a good time instead of sitting silently, trying to think of the next "right" thing to say. I don't think I've ever seen Frankie smile this much. When Sunshine returns to one of the loungers by the pool after eating, I follow along and lay next to him, the lounger barely big enough to hold us both. We lay there, skin to skin, and cuddle while his family enjoys themselves around us, and I finally feel like I'm home.

16

Despite living together and sharing the same bed, I feel like I hardly see Sunshine over the rest of the summer between classes and work. I'm so happy to finally have some time to breathe now that I've left Joe's again for the semester. Then again, even when we have seen each other, I can't quite seem to get past making out without feeling the familiar prickle of anxiety. Even in New York when he took me out for an incredibly romantic date on Broadway and we went back to the hotel, as soon as I reached for his waistband, warning signals lit up my brain.

Melissa has been invaluable. We've been working a lot through my child-hood, my need for perfection, and my relationship with my mom. Of course, I had wanted to bring up the issue between Sunshine and me before today, but I couldn't bring myself to talk about it out loud before.

Now, while Sunshine and I sit at the dinner table, Melissa's words from earlier are ringing in my ears. I know I have to talk to Sunshine about it, but I also know it's going to be one of the most uncomfortable conversations of my life. What if he decides I'm too damaged and he doesn't want me anymore? When I look up, Sunshine is giving me a look of curiosity with a smile.

"Instead of spiraling internally, let's just talk about whatever is going on in your beautiful mind," he says, reading me like a freaking book and turning my cheeks red.

How does he do that?

"Melissa and I talked about James today..." I start, gauging his reaction. He nods, silently urging me to continue. "I guess I always thought our relationship was amazing, but then Melissa started asking questions and... well it wasn't."

"Okay... tell me more?" He asks, placing a comforting hand on my thigh.

"I know Skye told you a little bit, but I hadn't come to terms with it quite yet. I see now that he was... pretty manipulative. He played my insecurities against me and made me completely dependent on him," I huff out a breath. "He, um..."

I look at Sunshine, knowing that this will change everything. That he'll never see me the same way again. His eyes are soft and he's holding my hand now, rubbing the back of it with his thumb.

"There are things that I did that I'm not proud of."

"You can tell me anything, Mia. I'm here, and I'm not going anywhere," he reassures.

"I talked to her about my... inability towards intimacy with you. Like, obviously I'm attracted to you, and you've never been anything short of amazing, so I want to keep taking steps to deepen our connection, but every time I get this like... internal panic. That's how we got on the subject of James. He's two years older than me and we started dating when I was like... fourteen? He had a really high sex drive, even then, but mine was... nonexistent. He talked a lot about wanting more."

"What a dick," he scoffs, anger contorting his face.

"I gave him a hand job like a month into dating so he'd just stop talking about it. Of course, that made it worse and then I'd have to do that often... I wasn't even sure I *wanted* to be in a relationship with him at the time, but my mom was so happy that we were together, and there wasn't a lot I did to make her happy at the time. He kept telling me, you know, how other girls would be excited to have sex with him and that's what good girlfriends did..."

I look over to Sunshine, frowning.

"There's nothing you can say, short of saying you hate me, that's going to push me away," Sunshine reassures me and I smile softly.

"It... got worse over the years. The hand jobs held him off for a little while, but when I was like seventeen he kept pushing for more. He kept saying that if I couldn't give it to him then he'd have to seek it out elsewhere and he didn't want to do that. I was kneeling down on the floor folding clothes and he just kind of stood over me with his dick out..." I look around the room. "I thought it was just a joke and I laughed it off, but he was smiling down at me and brought my hand up to him. He told me that it hurt. That he needed more than my hand. He moved my head toward it and that was that."

"And you didn't want to?" He asks, clarifying and looking at me with no hint of judgement.

"I mean, I told him I was uncomfortable. I didn't want him to hurt though," I say, "When I was done, he was still complaining about needing more, but I didn't want to give him everything."

"How did he react?" Sunshine asks.

"He thought I was joking and laughed it off. Then he threw me on the bed and started kissing me, but I pushed him off and left. He just kept trying every time we would do anything," I say. "And when I told Melissa about it... she mentioned sexual assault and asked if it was possible that that's what this was. I didn't think so, because I never really said no necessarily... but after talking with her a bit longer about it, I realized that it was. He sexually assaulted me. Several times."

Tears are starting to fall in quick succession as I look up at Sunshine. He's no longer looking at me, and his back teeth are clenching together so hard I can see it defined on his jaw.

"You're disgusted," I say through my tears.

"What? With you?" He looks at me, his eyes haunted. "Never."

I can't keep from crying. I always assumed if I had been assaulted, I would have known. How could I have been so naive?

"I'm so sorry," I say to Sunshine and put my head in my hands.

"Mia, look at me." He says, gently grabbing my wrist. I look at him through my tears. "I'm here. I'm following your pace, always. There is no world where I will make you do anything that you don't want to. Thank you, for trusting me with this."

When he pulls me into his chest, I cry harder. I feel so stupid.

"I'm sorry I didn't tell you. I think on some level I knew that my relationship with James was unhealthy, but I didn't think I let it get that bad."

"You did absolutely nothing wrong," he says, wiping away tears and cradling me against him. "No more apologizing for the actions of a complete asshole."

He continues to hold me for several moments until I'm able to calm myself down with the assistance of his steady heartbeat.

"Melissa gave me homework for this week," I say, my cheeks burning. "I've um... I've never really explored that part of myself, even alone. She said if I did it could help me gain some control and empowerment over it. I'm was thinking about going to go out with Skye tonight to process everything... is that ok with you?"

"However you need to heal is fine by me. And I just want to say for absolute clarity— I will never, *never* pressure you into something you don't want. I respect your boundaries. I'm willing to wait as long as you need." Sunshine smiles down at me. "You just tell me what you need from me."

"Just don't treat me differently, okay? I still want to feel wanted by you. Don't censor yourself."

"Easy," he nods. "Because I'll always want you."

After we finish eating, I head to my room to get ready while he plays a game in the living room. When I walk back out, Sunshine pauses his game and looks over at me.

"You look hot," he smiles.

"Thanks," I blush and he walks over to me.

"I'll miss you tonight," he says and kisses me.

"I can stay home?" I offer.

"No, no. Go spend time with Skye. I'm sure she misses the hell out of you. I can't keep you all to myself," he smiles down at me.

"She wanted to go to the club," I give a disgusted look.

"Let me know if you guys need a ride home," he smiles, "You'll have fun."

"Mr. Parker, are you suggesting I drink? *Underage?*" I feign shock.

"I'm suggesting you have a good time," he laughs. "If that involves alcohol so be it. Just don't get caught. I'll bail you out if I have to but I really don't want to have to. My bed will be waiting for you when you get home."

"I talked her into a movie night instead," I say. "And I think I'm going to try and sleep in my room again tonight."

"If that's what you want," he nods, "But my bed is still open if you're not there yet."

Skye is right on time. I tell her about my counseling session and the sexual assault revelation nearly as soon as I get in the car, unable to keep it from her, as she drives to our favorite restaurant.

"Oh. My. God," She says, "I could literally kill him. Can I kill him? He better hope I never fucking see him again."

"Stop," I say, "It's the past."

"No but for real, I could actually kill him and I'm a little disappointed that Sunshine hasn't gotten to him yet," She brushes it off. "So what do you do now?"

"I don't know... Melissa suggested that I, you know, do some *self-care*."

"Self-care?" She asks, confused and I give her an embarrassed look. "Oh. Wait, you weren't already? I figured being around someone like Sunshine so much you'd be doing that like... every night."

"No, I've never... you've met my mom," I say, eyebrows raised accusingly.

"Wait... you've *never* masturbated?" She nearly yells.

"Skye, oh my God. Stop. Shut up." I blush and frantically look around the restaurant to make sure no one has heard.

"Why?" She asks.

"I don't- I- Ugh. This is so embarrassing," I put my head in my hands.

"Okay, forget movie night, we're going to a sex shop."

"What? No. No way in hell."

"I'm just saying, I have a *little* experience in this area. I know what feels good and I know what makes other girls feel good. I'm just trying to help you follow your counselor's suggestion." She smiles at me suggestively.

"Isn't that weird though? Shouldn't I like... go by myself?"

"Not weird at all. Sex is not weird, masturbation is not weird, and you are not weird for wanting to do things with your hot as hell boyfriend," she reassures me, "Plus, how else are you going to know what you like and what you don't like if you don't explore it for yourself?"

I think on it a moment as I chew. On one hand, Skye is probably the person I'd be most comfortable going with, if only marginally. On the other hand, there's still that guilt put in place by my mother that's nagging at me. I know she's right— sex is normal, but it just feels so taboo.

"Okay, fine," I concede. "I'd rather go with someone that knows what they're doing and I *definitely* don't want to have to ask the people working."

When we walk into the sex shop it's nothing like I imagined. I pictured something... I don't know, dingy? With whips and chains hanging from the ceiling? This is more like... a normal store.

"Okay, wait, you'll love this one." Skye said, handing me something shaped like a rose.

"What the hell do I do with it?" I ask and blush as she whispers the answer in my ear.

"That one may be a bit too intense for you right away though," She says. "Here let's get that and... ooh a wand. And maybe a butterfly vibrator... I think that'll be good for the first visit."

"That's... a lot." I say.

"Girl this is like a quarter of my collection," she laughs.

Thank God I've never stumbled upon that. Wait, *how* have I never stumbled upon that?

"It would be my honor to purchase your first sexy time toys." Skye smiles at me as she whips her credit card out at the clerk.

"Can we still have our movie night?" I ask as we get back in the car.

"But of course!" She says, "I feel like I never see you anymore."

"Well I definitely don't want to become one of *those* girls," I say.

"Nah, you've been through a lot. I get it. Just don't forget about your bestie," she laughs and I hug her while she drives.

"Never," I say.

~

When we pull up at Sunshine's house late, I clutch the bag to my chest. I can only hope he's sleeping so I don't have to share this with him quite yet, but the lights being on on the first floor squashes that hope.

"Hey babe!" Sunshine says, jumping up from the couch where he's playing video games with his friends.

"Hey," I say, still clutching the bag. "I'm going to head to my room."

"This is Tony and Greg. They're in the theater department, too," he says and I wave to them. I swear this man has more friends than anyone I've ever met. "How was movie night?"

"It was good," I say, "Just did some shopping first after dinner."

"Ooh, did you buy me anything?" He asks, pulling part of the bag back and looking inside.

I pull it back toward me quickly, but I know he's already seen the contents when he looks up at me with a sly smile.

"I'm going to catch a shower," I say, blushing.

"Okay," he kisses my forehead before he whispers in my ear, "Enjoy your shower."

I head to my room and shut and lock the door, dumping the contents on my bed. Where the hell do I start? Skye mentioned them all being waterproof, and it would probably be a good idea to have the shower there as background noise. Do I put music on, too? I take the bright pink, silicone wand out of it's box and fumble with the buttons as it hums to life. I quickly turn it off and head into the bathroom, putting the shower on to dim the noise as planned. There are a lot of different speeds and styles and I'm perplexed. I turn it off and turn it back on again, putting it on the lowest setting before stepping in the shower. I move it between my legs and nearly let out a moan at the overwhelming feeling. I put my hand on the shower wall and remove the wand. It's almost too much— feels too good. I take a moment to breathe before placing it carefully back on my clit and melting into the sensation. I lean my elbow against the wall to move my hand to my mouth, having a hard time keeping quiet. Everything feels so intense until the intenseness releases in a kind of explosion. I'm panting and smiling to myself when I let out a small laugh. *That's* what I've been missing? How did I go so long without that? I can't help but think about Sunshine... how would it feel if it was him and not a toy?

I get dressed slowly, still smiling to myself. I think of our last dinner with his family... how his abs looked soaking wet and the way he smiled at me when he saw me in my bikini... I grab the wand again and lay in bed with it. This feeling could easily become an addiction.

Once I'm fully satisfied, I leave my room. Sunshine is on the couch playing video games, but he's alone now. How long have I been in there?

"How was your shower?" He asks, pausing the game and looking at me.

"It was... amazing," I blush and he smiles.

"I bet it was," he laughs shaking his wet hair.

"Did you shower, too?" I ask.

"Yeah," he lets out a small laugh. "The guys left shortly after you got home and the thought of you... I had to shower."

"How often do you, uh, 'shower?'" I ask.

"Pretty much every day... when I shower," he laughs. "Especially since you moved in."

"What do you think about?" I ask.

"Always you," he responds in all seriousness.

"Can I try something?" I ask.

"Yeah, of course," he says.

I move my hands to the hem of my shirt and take it off slowly. It's late so I didn't put a bra on. He stands, moving one hand to my hip, and looks at me.

"Fuck, you're beautiful," he says.

I move my hands to the hem of his shirt and take a deep breath, pushing away the rising anxiety. He helps me take it off of him. I stare at his chest and then wrap my arms around his waist in a hug. He holds me and kisses the top of my head. I move back again and slowly take my shorts off, careful to leave my underwear on for now. When I move to take his shorts off and feel the familiar anxiety rising, I picture James standing over me, coaxing me. I look off to the side, my hands still at his waistband.

"I'm here," he whispers, pulling me back to reality. "Following your lead. There's no pressure."

I take a breath and slowly pull his shorts down, leaving his boxers on.

"You're so beautiful," he whispers, moving closer to me.

I lead him to the couch and softly push him down before straddling his lap.

"Are you okay?" He asks and I nod.

I kiss him softly. His hands trail up and down my back, soothing me. I move to kiss his neck and a breath escapes him. He moves his hands to my waist and keeps them planted there. I move his hand to my chest and throw my head back as he rolls one of my nipples between his fingers. He kisses my neck and I moan. Sunshine grows hard beneath me, only thin fabric between us, and I see James with his head thrown back as I suck on him. I try to push the image away but I can't. Sunshine lets out a small moan and I feel like I'm going to be sick.

"Fuck," I shout standing up, my eyes filling with tears.

I gather my clothes and head to my room, quickly getting dressed and lying in my bed.

"Mia," I hear from the other side of the door followed by a soft knock.

"Not now, Sunshine," I cry.

"Please?" He begs.

"Come in," I sigh.

He's fully dressed again and walks to my bed slowly, sitting on the edge.

"What happened?" he asks.

"I couldn't... I keep having these like... flashbacks?" I say, embarrassed. "I'm so pissed at myself."

"Flashbacks... to what he did to you?" he asks and I nod.

"I want you," I cry, "I don't want to be this way."

"I know, baby. It's okay. Can I hold you?" he asks and I nod.

He cuddles up behind me, spooning me and playing with my hair.

"I want you too," he whispers, "In every way. But I'm in no hurry."

He lies with me until I fall asleep.

17

"Come on Mia, show me how much you love me," James's voice groans as he pushes my head towards his dick.

"James..." I start, "I'm not ready."

"If you really loved me, you'd want to make me feel good. I need it, Mia."

I feel tears hot on my cheeks. I can't do this. I don't want to do this. I feel like I'm going to throw up.

"Come on, you'll love it," he coaxes. "And it's been so long since you touched it."

He moves my hand to touch him.

"Come on baby," he cradles my face. "Don't make me find someone that will."

I can't lose him. My whole world would crumble. I put my mouth around him and do as I'm told. He tastes of sweat and he forces himself so far in that I gag.

I shoot to an upright position on the bed with a gasp and sob. I don't even remember falling asleep.

"Baby, baby," Sunshine holds me, "What's wrong?"

I turn to face him and touch his face, making sure he's real.

"I just, he..." I sob.

"It's me," he soothes, "I'm here. He can't hurt you."

"It was a nightmare," I say, "But it put me right back there."

"Do you want to talk about it?" He asks.

"He... I told him I wasn't ready. I was crying." I cry.

"He'll never touch you again," he reassures me. "You're safe."

I sob and he runs his fingers through my hair. He sings "Perfect" by Ed Sheeran and it calms me until I fall asleep again, wrapped in his arms.

"Mia..." he rubs the side of my face to wake me. "Mia, baby."

"Mmm," I smile with my eyes closed and then remember what happened last night.

"I'm sorry," I frown.

"No, no, where did that smile go?" He smiles down at me. "Stop being sorry. I'm here no matter what."

I smile at him again and he kisses my forehead.

"I made you breakfast."

This man is the complete opposite of what I'm used to in the absolute best way. I kiss his cheek and hop on his back, getting a piggyback ride to the kitchen.

"What are your opinions on dogs?" I ask him, sitting on the breakfast bar.

"Love them," he says. "Why?"

"Can we get one?" I ask. "I mean can I? Can I get one?"

"Yeah, *we* can get one." He smiles.

"I just think it might make it more comfortable to sleep in my bed," I say.

"Can I ask why you're so adamant about sleeping in there?" He asks. "We've slept together every night for months now."

"It's too soon," I say.

"Says who?" He asks.

"I don't know... society? I just don't want you to think I'm some freeloader." I shrug.

"I wouldn't ever think that. I want you here. And I want you in my bed. We can put some of your stuff in the room too if that makes you feel better about it? We can redecorate and make it feel more like both of ours..." he says.

"It's important to me that I can sleep without you again," I say.

"If I have my way it would never happen again, but I respect it. You want to go look today? There's a rescue up the road."

I nod quickly, like a kid who's been asked if they want to take a trip to the candy store.

When we walk through the doors of the rescue, I want to adopt every single animal I lay eyes on. There's a ton of puppies, a few cats, and a big, blue nose pit bull in the corner, cowering. I point him out to Sunshine and smile.

"Can we see him?" He asks the worker.

"Absolutely!" She says. "This is Romeo. He's three. As you can imagine, he's been passed over by so many families and he's been with us for about a year. He's very affectionate, just somewhat apprehensive to strangers. No history with aggression, but he'd probably do best in a house as the only pet."

"Is he good with kids?" I ask and Sunshine looks at me confused. "You know, for when we have Birdie or Frankie over?"

"He's great with kids," she smiles.

She brings us to an open area to meet him and brings him in on a leash. I sit cross-legged on the floor and Sunshine follows suit.

"Hi Romeo," I smile at him.

Romeo tilts his head at the mention of his name and then slowly walks over to me, sniffing my legs and hands. When he's decided he's smelled me enough, his tail goes crazy. I smile and let him sniff my hand before petting him. As soon as my hand hits his head, he lays on his back and puts his head in my lap.

"Wow, there have been a lot of families that have spent time with him but this is the first time I've seen him take to someone so quickly."

I look at Sunshine, smiling.

"Well, clearly this is her dog," he laughs, "We'll take him."

Sunshine fills out the adoption paperwork while I spend more time with Romeo. He lets me hug him and licks my face. Sunshine walks back over with a collar, leash, and a big bag of dog food.

"Do you want to go to the pet store and pick some things out for him?" He asks.

When he reaches down to pet Romeo, he leans into his hand to get scratches. Who wouldn't want this dog?

"Aww he loves you," I smile. "Yeah, let's go."

Romeo is so well-mannered in the store, but shy to others. We pick out way too many toys, treats, and other various supplies, so long as they had Romeo's stamp of approval. When we get home, Romeo makes himself comfortable on the couch, laying his head in my lap after I sit.

"He thinks he's a lap dog," Sunshine laughs and sits next to me. He kisses me.

"Is he okay on the furniture?" I ask.

"Yeah, of course. I love dogs. And I love him." He keeps petting him and Romeo falls asleep in my lap.

"Yeah, me too. He's the cutest. So sweet." I lean down and kiss Romeo.

"I get the feeling you're not coming to my bed tonight," he frowns.

"That's kind of the plan, yeah..." I trail.

"I just don't know if *I* can sleep without *you* now," he laughs. "I guess I'll have to manage."

"Thank you for letting me get a dog," I say.

"Are you kidding? I saw you look at him. There was no way we were leaving without him."

I look at him and smile.

"Oh hey, your birthday is coming up. Any idea what you might like to do?" He asks.

"I don't know," I say. "It's a school night."

"We can't do nothing!" He says. "I'll think of something. Skye and I have a few ideas already."

"I'm not a big birthday person," I say.

"Of course you're not," he laughs.

"What does that mean?" I ask.

"It's something that celebrates you. Of course you don't like it."

"It's not like it's a big deal," I say.

"I disagree wholeheartedly. You deserve to feel special and you deserve to be celebrated." He kisses my cheek. "I think I'm going to head to bed."

"Okay," I smile. "I'm going to stay up a bit longer and read."

"Have sweet dreams, I'm right upstairs if you need anything."

"Thanks," I smile at him.

When I move to my book nook to read, Romeo follows, laying on the floor next to me. When I move to the bedroom to go to sleep, he's right behind me again, laying right next to me on the bed. I'm starting to think this dog needs me as much as I need him. I'm lying in the dark when my phone chirps with a text message.

> I miss you in my bed :(

> I miss you more <3

Romeo's snuggles are great. The best dog snuggles I've ever had for sure, but I miss Sunshine's snuggles. The way he'd wrap his arms around me tightly... the way I'd press into him on a stretch in the mornings and find him rock hard.

I shoo Romeo off of the bed temporarily, grabbing my wand from my nightstand and close my eyes. I'm going to need to get over this intimacy issue bullshit soon, because I need to feel his hands on me.

When I finish, I invite Romeo back up and turn some soft music on my phone before petting him until I fall asleep. The nightmares continue their assault. Exact replicas of my encounters with James, except now when I wake in a sweat, Romeo licks my face and I pet him until I fall asleep again.

18

When my alarm goes off Romeo jumps off the bed and heads straight for the back door, so I let him out and start on breakfast.

"You made it in your bed." Sunshine walks into the kitchen in only pajama bottoms, rubbing his eyes.

"I did." I smile and nod. "I'm making pancakes."

"Mmm, my own little homemaker," he comes up behind me and wraps his arms around my waist. I laugh and turn to face him.

"It helped that I was able to... turn my brain off for a bit," I say.

"How so?" He asks and I smile, blushing. "*Oh*. Don't do that to me."

He smiles down at me and kisses me.

"Why? Are you going to need a shower?" I giggle.

"I swear, I'm going to need multiple showers if you keep walking around in these shorts." He slowly slides his hands down to my ass and I smile.

"I've noticed something." I say.

"What's that?" He asks.

"When you touch me... I don't feel as much anxiety. It's only when I touch you." I say, embarrassed.

"Oh really?" He raises his eyebrows. "That makes sense though if he never did anything *to* you."

"Yeah I guess," I sigh. "It just sucks because I want to make you feel good."

"Mmm, making you feel good makes me feel good." He smiles.

"Can we try something?" I ask.

"Always," he says, kissing a trail down my neck to my shoulder.

"I should probably finish breakfast first," I say, turning back to the stove, but Sunshine reaches over and turns the burner off.

"I'm not that hungry anyways."

I giggle and pull him down to kiss me, our tongues mingling together. I guide his hands up my body and he rolls one of my nipples through my shirt. I back away, taking a breath, and quickly strip my shirt and shorts off. Sunshine takes in my body before taking his shirt off and claiming my mouth again.

"I'll tell you if I get uncomfortable, I promise." I whisper and he nods. He sinks to his knees and runs his hands up and down my sides as he puts one of my nipples in his mouth, lightly sucking before gently biting.

"Oh God," I pant, looking down at him.

He looks up at me for my reaction and smiles smugly. He kisses down my stomach, moving one hand to a breast and the other rubbing up and down my leg.

He sucks briefly on one of my hips as he moves his hand up to my upper thigh.

I bite my lip and watch as his fingers slip below the thin fabric of my underwear, looking up at me as if asking for permission. When I nod, he stands and kisses me passionately as his fingers work over my clit. I moan and put my hand on his shoulder to steady myself. I feel like I'm going to collapse right before I release and let out a small laugh. That was *so* much better than my toy. He kisses me again and again with soft, loving kisses.

"Are you okay?" he whispers, after I've come down fully. "How are you feeling?"

"Um... euphoric? Yeah, that seems like a good enough word." I laugh.

"I love the sounds you make." He kisses my neck and I want more.

I feel him through his pajama pants and he's rock hard. He looks at me.

"I think you've pushed yourself far enough for today. There is no tit for tat." He smiles at me and kisses me again.

I frown at him. But I know he's right. I don't want to ruin it.

"Can we do that again soon?" I ask and he smiles.

"Literally whenever you want." He kisses me again. "I'm going to have to take a shower. Probably a long shower. You are so incredibly sexy."

"I may have to take one too," I laugh.

"Just don't have too much fun without me," he hugs me. "Thank you for trusting me."

I smile up at him and kiss him again, then watch as he heads up the stairs to his room. I finish up a few pancakes before turning the stove off and letting Romeo in, heading up the stairs after him and knocking on his bathroom door.

"What's up, babe? Everything okay?" He calls out.

"Can I come in?" I ask.

"I mean, I'm in the shower."

"I know."

"Sure?" He laughs.

When I walk in, he's in the shower in the corner, the glass frosted from his waist down. His hair is down in his face, but he pushes it back to look at me, concerned.

"Are you okay?" He asks.

Fuck, those abs.

"Yeah, I just wanted to see how it would feel to see you naked..." I say, "is that okay? Is that weird?"

"Totally okay and not weird at all," he says with a shy smile.

I strip down to my underwear and open the shower door, stepping in with him. His body is....indescribable. It's gorgeous, beautiful, immaculate... except none of those words are enough. He's still partially hard, his dick red as if he's just finished getting himself off and he lets out a nervous laugh.

"Am I making you nervous?" I ask.

"A little?" He laughs. "Not in a bad way. I've just not been this intimate with anyone."

"You've had sex..." I say, confused.

"Yeah, but intimacy doesn't always mean sex and sex doesn't always have to be intimate. A lot of the women I've had sex with I hardly knew... lots of one night stands. And then there was Natalie, but I didn't have the same connection with her. We are a lot more... intense? But in the best way? I don't know how to explain it." He says.

"I get it," I nod, "I feel it too."

I wrap my arms around his waist and rest my head on his chest, the water hitting both of us. After listening to his heart beat against my cheek for several moments, I step away from him and shimmy slowly out of my underwear.

"You are so breathtakingly beautiful," he says, taking in the sight of me.

When I walk back over to him, I get on my tip toes and kiss him. The way he kisses me back, his hands on my waist steadying me, is so sweet I could almost cry.

"I love you, Mia," he whispers when he breaks the kiss, kissing my forehead now.

I know there's no pressure to say it back. He's never pressured me into anything. Could it actually be love? It still feels too soon to tell. I know I never want to lose him, but is that love? Or infatuation?

We embrace in the shower until the water starts to turn cold, exchanging kisses every now and again.

"Will you please sleep in my bed with me?" He asks. "You proved to yourself you can sleep without me, now can we stop torturing ourselves?"

"Yeah, fuck it," I smile. "I'll move some of my stuff upstairs too."

"So we're sharing a room now?" He asks.

"Yeah yeah, I'll take over your room if you really want me to." I laugh.

"Can we get out of the shower now though? I think I felt one of my balls retreat into my body," he laughs and I nod.

"I need to get ready for work anyways," I say, grabbing a towel for both of us.

"If you already had your clothes up here in *our* room, you wouldn't have to leave me to do so." He kisses my cheek and then lightly slaps my ass. "But you don't, so go get ready."

I feel lighter than air as I walk through the campus to the library. It feels so good to finally be getting my shit figured out. I'm on a gorgeous campus, studying something *I* want to, all alongside my best friend and an incredibly attractive man who just told me he *loves* me. Love. But how can he be sure?

Nope. Not going down that road today, I'm too happy. No "twisty spirally" today, as Skye would say. His feelings are his to figure out and if he says he loves me, I believe him. I've never moved this fast in a relationship, not that I have that much experience, but I'm so happy I can't overthink it.

"Mimi!" A familiar voice calls out.

Of course James has to ruin it. What the fuck is he doing on campus? Am I dreaming? My heart starts racing and my legs start shaking. I feel the need to run as far away from him as I can.

"Mimi!" he yells again, catching up to me. "I'm so glad I ran into you. I figured you'd probably be taking summer classes, you were always so committed."

He wraps me in a hug and I can't help but freeze against him.

"What are you doing here?" I ask.

"I came to apologize. I think there are some things we need to talk through. Can I take you for a coffee?" He asks.

"I have work," I say, walking through the doors of the library.

"I can wait. Do some studying. Please?" He asks.

"I'll think about it," I say.

"I'll be in that corner there studying," He points to a section of the library. "Come get me when you're done."

Once I'm safely in the office, I shoot a text to Sunshine.

> James is here... at the library.

> What? What the hell is he doing here? What the hell does he want?

> I don't know, but I have to clock in. Thank you for this morning.

> Trust me, the pleasure is all mine. I love you.

When I round the circulation desk, James is sitting off at a corner table in view. I can feel his eyes on me as I help fellow students find and check out books. I want more than anything to march over there and tell him just how unwelcome he is, but I can't convince myself to do it. Once there is a lull in students, he strides over to the circulation desk.

"Hey, you have a minute to talk?"

"Not really," I say. "I have a lot of work that needs to get done."

"Aww come on Mimi. Ten minutes."

The sound of the elevator startles me, but I look up to see Sunshine walk through. He stands behind James, forming a queue, patiently.

"Did you need help finding something? If not, I have a job to get back to."

"Come on, Mimi, promise you'll have a coffee with me after work. I'll wait."

Sunshine clears his throat from behind James. James turns to look at him and then turns back to me.

"Ten minutes. I want to apologize."

James steps to the side to allow Sunshine to approach the desk, as if he'll get what he needs and go. Sunshine leans over the desk to get closer to me, taking a quick look around for other employees before he places one hand on my cheek and plants a soft, tender kiss on my lips.

"Hey babe. I missed you."

I'm sure the look on James's face is worth it, but I have no desire to look anywhere but up at this amazing man, who seems to know what I need before even I do. Sunshine leans an arm on the desk and turns his attention to James.

"Oh, sorry man. Did you need something?" He asks, raising an eyebrow.

"Uh, no. I'm good. Nice to see you again." James bows his head slightly and heads back for his table in the corner.

"Thank you for coming."

"I'll be here as long as he is. What the hell is he even doing here?"

"He said he wants to get coffee when I get off. So he can apologize. If I know him, he's probably not going to fuck off until I hear him out. Not after he came all this way... Will you come with me?"

"I can't be nice to him," he says.

"Can you just be there? You don't have to say anything, nice or not," I say.

He lets out a long breath. "I don't like it, but I'll be there."

Sunshine offers another small kiss on my cheek before taking a seat at the table nearest the circulation desk, leg extended and pretending to read a book while keeping his eyes on the table James is at. Every so often during shift I catch James staring over at me, which prompts Sunshine to walk over and ask a random question. It's the most awkward shift of my life, but I am eternally grateful for Sunshine's presence.

Once I leave the office after clocking out, Sunshine is waiting for me with a giant hug.

"Waiting for you to get off of work is literal torture."

James idles awkwardly to the side, and I can imagine the smug look Sunshine is wearing as he faces him.

"Mimi?" He asks.

"Come on. There's a coffee shop on campus." I sigh.

19

The walk to the coffee shop is as awkward as possible, with the exception of Sunshine's hand in mine. We're all pretty silent throughout the walk, and Sunshine gets in line when we arrive.

"Do you want anything Mimi?" James asks, as he stands behind Sunshine in line.

"I've got her drink," he smiles back at him. "Thanks though."

Sunshine kisses my cheek as he takes a seat next to me and hands me my favorite cold brew. James takes a seat across from him, clearly unhappy with our being together, but I honestly couldn't care less.

"So listen," he starts. "Last time I was here I was a real asshole. I was just hurting really badly. I just miss you so much and I love you so much that I couldn't accept the breakup. I basically just wanted to say I'm sorry."

"Okay..." I say.

"How have you been since I last saw you? What's been going on?" He asks. "I'm so glad to see you happy."

"Thanks, we're really happy together," I say.

"We moved in together," Sunshine says. "Mia lives in my house now."

"Oh... nice. What happened to your apartment? Skye there alone now?" He asks.

"It was actually broken into and ransacked pretty badly," I say. "We couldn't stay there."

"Oh my gosh." James grabs my hand across the table. "Mia, I'm so sorry, are you okay?"

Sunshine picks James hand up by his fingers, removing it and replacing it with his.

"She's fine," he says, and I place my other hand on his thigh under the table.

"I'm sorry," James says. "I forgot you have a new man to speak for you now."

"I speak for myself," I say, offended.

"I didn't mean it like that," James says. "I'm sorry. I must seem like a real jackoff."

"Because you are," Sunshine says under his breath.

"I'm sorry, what was that?" James asks.

"Oh I said because you are," Sunshine smiles at him.

"Guys please... let's not make a scene," I say.

"You don't even know me," James scoffs.

"I know enough," Sunshine says.

"Yeah? What is it you know?" James asks.

"I know what you did to her. And you're lucky that I respect her enough to be civil," Sunshine says.

Oh no. No no no. This can't happen. Not here. Not in public.

"What did you tell him?" James looks at me and I look away, unable to form a thought.

"I think we're done here," Sunshine stands and puts a hand out for me.

"What the hell did you tell him Mia?!" James asks.

I feel the stares of other coffee shop patrons starting through me and my heart speeds up and my stomach sours.

"Okay, okay," I stand and take Sunshine's hand. "Sunshine's right. We should go."

"There are still things we need to talk about," James says.

"I'd rather not have an audience," I say.

I follow Sunshine out of the coffee shop, holding his hand tightly, when I feel James tug on my arm.

"Dude, get your fucking hands off of her." Sunshine steps between us.

"She's my *friend,* man. I'm just trying to talk to her." James sizes Sunshine up.

"Your *friend*? Dude, for real? After what you did?" Sunshine scowls.

"What the hell did you tell him?" James shouts, looking at me. "Tell me, Mia!"

"You should be in jail, you piece of shit," Sunshine says. "You will *never* touch her again."

I tug Sunshine towards the car with tears in my eyes, before he can say any more.

"Please," I say, "Please let's go."

Sunshine follows me to the car and holds my face in both hands when I get to the passenger side.

"Are you okay?" He asks.

"I'm fine!" I say, swatting his hands away and getting in the car. "Let's just go."

"Are you pissed at me?" He asks after getting in the driver's side.

"Why would you say any of that to him?" I ask.

"I told you I couldn't be nice," he scoffs.

"It is my decision if I confront him about the assault or not! Not yours! It happened to *me*, Sunshine. Not you." I say.

"I know that! Of course I know that. I just..." he sighs, "I don't understand I guess. Why would you even want to see him after what he did to you? It's like he still has some weird pull on you."

"Excuse me?" I fume.

"I didn't mean it like that."

As soon as he parks the car in the driveway, I get out and slam the door behind me, storming into the house and straight to my room, calling Romeo after me.

"Mia?" He's knocking at the door.

"What?" I snap.

"Come on babe, talk to me. I'm sorry. I didn't mean to make you uncomfortable."

I stomp over to the door and swing it open.

"It's not even that! You forced me into talking about it *with* him! You really think he's just going to let it go?!"

A look of horror crosses his face as the words come out of my mouth and he tries to take my hand, but I pull it away.

"Oh God, Mia. Oh my God, I'm so sorry. I didn't think of it that way. Please forgive me."

"I just need some time to cool off," I say. "And figure out how I'm going to deal with this."

"Let me help, please. I can... I'll talk to him about it. I'll be as civil as I can, promise. Please tell me how I can fix this."

"You can't." I shake my head. "Just don't say anything else. I'm going to stay in here tonight."

"Okay." He hangs his head. "I love you."

I pout in response and close the door softly.

I hate that he's hurting, but I also hate what he did. I know he had the best intentions but that shit was uncalled for. I'm not sure I was ever going to talk with James about what he did, but now I have to. My phone chimes with an incoming text message from a number that isn't saved in my phone, but I know by heart. How did he get my new number?

> Trouble in paradise?

He must have seen my rejection to Sunshine at the car.

> No, we're great.

> Mia, we need to talk.

> I have nothing to say to you.

> Clearly you do.

I leave him on read and Romeo licks my face, sensing that something is off. I cry and hug him until I fall asleep.

When I walk into the kitchen, I'm hit with the smell of bacon and eggs, and there are a dozen roses and my favorite candies sitting on the breakfast bar. When he notices I've walked in the room, Sunshine abandons the food and moves to me, hugging me around the waist.

"I'm so sorry," he says. "Please, please forgive me. I promised I'd never force you into anything and I did without even thinking."

"I forgive you. I don't want to fight."

I hug him back and the tension leaves his body.

"I know what I want to do though."

"What's that?"

"I need to talk to him about it. Face it head on. I want to do it at the park, since it's still public but there won't be as many people, and I want you to be there."

"Okay." He nods. "Okay, yes I'll be there."

"But you can't say anything. I mean it, not a word."

"Mia come on... The dude's an asshole. He's going to say some shit that'll piss me off."

"And you'll let me handle it."

"Fine. I don't like it, but I'll do it. For you." He sighs.

We settle on meeting later in the day, and I wear the baggiest clothes I can find. Something about him being able to see my body clearly after I realized what he did to me feels nauseating.

"Mia." James smiles and moves to hug me when he sees me, but I turn to the side.

"James," I say, cordially.

"I'm glad you wanted to meet again. Even if you brought your bodyguard."

"He's just here for support. This is between you and me. Say what you need to say."

"Yeah so... I was coming to see you to let you know I'm moving back here. I'm dropping out of Duke and enrolling at Eastview."

"What? Why?"

"Well, no offense to you, Sunshine, but this isn't over." He looks at Sunshine and gestures between us.

"This is definitely over," I respond, shaking my head.

"I can be better, Mimi. I promise. I can be the man you need," he says, placing a gentle hand on my arm.

When I look over at Sunshine, he's looking off to the side and his jaw is tense. This has to be torture for him— not being able to say anything.

"You can't, because you're not him," I say, still looking at Sunshine for a moment before turning my gaze back to James.

"You can't be serious. You want to be serious with a guy named *Sunshine?* For real?"

"I don't want you here, James. I don't want to be around you."

"Come on, you don't mean that," he says and puts a hand on my shoulder but I shrug him off.

"Stop touching me." I feel a rage building inside me. "Never touch me again."

"Mimi..."

"And don't call me that! Don't transfer here, I don't want you here. Don't you get it? I left Duke to get away from *you*."

"You love me. Remember?"

"No, I don't love you." I take a breath. "I'm sorry, but I never did."

His face contorts in a way I'd seen only a few times from him— a way that I can only describe as evil.

"Yeah? Then why did you suck me off, huh?" He moves closer to me. "Why did you touch me if you didn't love me back? Let's not lie just because your boyfriend is here, Mia."

I push him back with more force than I knew I was even capable of.

"You *assaulted* me. You *knew* I didn't want to," I yell, tears in my eyes. "You manipulated and guilted me into it!"

"Is that the bullshit you told him? You loved it. You loved every second. You *begged* for it. Don't lie to spare his feelings You were always so horny. So needy."

"It's not true," I shake my head and he walks toward me. I walk backward, the fire I just had quickly melting into fear.

"Come here, I'll remind you," he grips my hand hard and I look to Sunshine for help, feeling nearly paralyzed in place.

Sunshine's face is filled with pure, unfiltered rage as he places one firm hand on James's shoulder and the other on his wrist of the arm that's holding mine.

"That's enough. I don't want to go to jail today."

"I'm not giving up, Mia. We belong together and you know it." He shrugs Sunshine's hand off.

"I hate you," I say, shaking my head. "I never want to see you again."

"You're going to have a hard time with that when I'm in all of your classes. Did I mention I'm changing my major, too?" James says, smiling wickedly.

"I swear James if you transfer here, I *will* press charges and I *will* file a restraining order. It'll be really hard to get *any* job with a sexual assault charge on your record." I threaten.

"You wouldn't," he challenges.

"Don't fucking try me."

"Whatever." He scoffs and looks me up and down. "I can do way better than you anyways."

"Please do. And leave me the fuck alone." I'm shouting now and walking towards James, Sunshine grabbing my arm softly to stop me.

"Let's go home." He kisses the side of my head and drops his voice in a dangerous tone while he turns his head to look back at James. "Come near her again and you'll be in the hospital."

"Is that a threat?" James asks.

"Oh, it absolutely is," Sunshine says and interlaces his fingers with mine before walking toward the car.

"Are you okay?" He asks when we get in the car.

"That sucked. Hopefully he won't go through with it."

"I honestly doubt it. It was probably an empty threat. Something to fuck with you... I'm sorry I didn't stay quiet like I said I would."

"Don't be. You knew I needed you and I was so grateful for that," I kiss his hand as he drives.

"I love you, Mia."

20

"Rise and shine, gorgeous! First day of class and I've made a big breakfast for you *and* I packed you a lunch." Sunshine kisses me awake and I pull him on top of me.

When did he become such a morning person?

"Nooooo." I groan, kissing his neck and wrapping my legs around him. "Sleeeeep."

"Come on baby." He kisses my neck. "If you do really well in all of your classes today, I'll reward you tonight."

"Mmmmm, can't I cash it in early?"

"I wish, but I also have class to get to." He nibbles my ear and then kisses my lips. "Come on, you temptress."

I laugh and follow him down to the kitchen where Justin and Asher are sitting at the table, already eating.

"Thanks for breakfast, bro." Justin says, wolfing down pancakes.

"Mia, you look crabby. Sunshine, you better take your girl back upstairs and give her a better start to her morning." Asher jest, pointing to the stairs with his fork.

"That's what I'm saying," I mumble and take a bite of bacon, leaning on the kitchen table.

"If she had woken up thirty minutes ago when I tried then that would have been possible," Sunshine laughs and hands me a lunch box.

"Thanks, Dad," I tease and he shakes his head, smiling.

It feels so good to be starting a fresh semester on campus, even if Skye and Aubrey ditched me to graduate. Bitches. After a relaxing summer with the best boyfriend and the greatest friends in the world, I feel like I'm walking on cloud nine. Still, there's a pang of anxiety from James' threat. He wouldn't actually transfer would he?

> Remember what I said, be good today and you'll get a reward ;)

> I'll be on my best behavior!

When I look up, I see him sitting in front of me. My palms start sweating and my breath quickens. There's no way. But I'd recognize the back of his head anywhere. Of course I can't make a scene in the middle of the classroom. Not when I'm still trying to get to know my classmates. I take a few deep breaths and try to focus on class.

"Mia! How was your summer?" Aisling, a fellow education major, asks.

"It was fine. Great actually. My boyfriend and I moved in together and had a great summer. How was yours?" I ask, trying to keep my breaths even.

"Not as good as yours it sounds like!" She laughs. "What about you Luke?"

James turns his head to look at Aisling. He went through all that trouble to change his name? What the fuck?

"It was alright."

"Have you met Luke yet, Mia? He wasn't in our class last semester, but he's a fellow education major." Aisling says and James turns to face me... and it's not James at all. I breathe a small sigh of relief.

"No, I haven't. I'm Mia."

I was *sure* that was him. I'm losing it. I take a breath and try to focus on the rest of the school day, trying to remind myself of what's waiting at home.

"How were classes?" Sunshine asks as I walk through the door.

"Good."

"That was an awfully loaded 'good.' What's on your mind?"

"I don't want to talk about it right now. I just want you to make my brain shut off for a little while."

"Can do." He smiles seductively, leading me up to our room and making good on his promise.

~

"Happy birthday Mia," Sunshine whispers, cuddling me from behind and stroking my hair to wake me.

"Mmm," I groan. "I hate birthdays."

"I know, I know, but Skye said you told her you'd meet her at the coffee shop before classes." He kisses my cheek and then my neck.

"I did," I groan. "But I just want to sleeeeeep."

"I know," I feel his smile on my neck.

He moves his hands up and down my side and then moves to my leg. His hand trails my inner thigh before moving to my waistband and I'm squirming.

"Okay, maybe not sleep, but I definitely want to be in bed," I breathe.

"I have your first birthday present." He kisses my neck again, sucking slightly. "Do you want it now or later?"

"Definitely now." My breath hitches.

"You'll stop me if you need to?" He asks.

"Promise."

He takes his time, feeling me through my clothes and I let out a gasp. I didn't even realize that I missed his touch and it's literally been 12 hours since I last had it. I may not be able to move past this, but he definitely makes sure to tend to me often. He slowly moves his hands up to my waistband and pulls my shorts down, taking my underwear with it. His palm covers me, his fingers lightly dancing along my clit, teasing, and I can hardly take it. I stifle a moan.

"Oh come on." His breath is hot on my ear and then softly bites it. "That's one of my favorite parts."

"We have roommates." I squirm. "Roommates that are actually awake this time."

"Trust me, I've listened to them enough. Plus they're allllll the way downstairs."

My hips move to the rhythm of his fingers, as if I'm not controlling them, and I let out a small moan. Between his fingers hooking inside me and his thumb taking it's cues from me, alternating between soft and hard pressure on my clit, I couldn't hold my moans in even if I wanted to. It doesn't take long for my release to rush in and I let out a long, loud moan.

I'm a pile of mush. Boneless. Truly.

Sunshine shifts to hover over me, smiles down at me, and kisses my neck again. He moves down my body to my breasts and sucks on a nipple before continuing down.

"What are you—?" I pant, lifting the blankets to see him.

"Do you want me to stop?" He looks up at me with a smile with a smile.

I look down at him, panting and nervous as hell. This is normal. It's been weeks of just touching and I want to move in the direction of actually being able to do something for him... Most women love it and it *is* my birthday after all. Fuck it.

"No." I breathe. "Don't stop."

He kisses small sweet kisses on my thighs before I feel his tongue graze me. I twitch, still in overdrive from the last orgasm and hear him let out a small laugh before tasting me again. His tongue swirls around my clit as he hooks his fingers back inside me, his other hand gripping firmly on my hip to keep me in place. Before now I had thought for sure that I had already had the biggest and best orgasm of my life, but he proves me wrong as I come around his tongue.

"You taste..." he kisses back up my body. "So good."

I kiss his neck, feeling like I'll never be fully satisfied.

"I need to shower now," he says with a huge smile.

I don't think I've ever seen him happier.

"Can I come?" I ask.

"I do believe you just did." He laughs and wiggles his eyebrows suggestively. "No for real though, I need to *shower.*"

"So?" I pout. "I want to come too."

"Oh don't do that to me," he smiles and hugs me while standing, my head on his chest where I plant small kisses. "You're already late to coffee with Skye. If you still want to, we can shower together tonight."

"Fine." I whine, elongating the word.

"I love you, Mia. So much. Happy birthday." He kisses the top of my head and heads for the bathroom.

I clean myself up and get dressed quickly, before heading downstairs.

"Good morning, *roomie.*" Justin laughs

"Happy birthday," Asher says.

"Thanks."

"Sounds like you cashed in on a birthday present early," Justin teases.

"Oh my God, stop," I laugh, blushing. "I'm sorry."

"Don't be sorry for getting it," Asher laughs. "God knows our girls aren't quiet either."

I check my phone for the time and am already running fifteen minutes late to meeting up with Skye.

"Okay. Yeah. Cool. Bye now." I laugh awkwardly.

When I get to the coffee shop, it's easy to spot Skye with the giant bouquet of balloons that sit at the table with her.

"Happy birthday Mi!!" She hugs me when I approach, and hands me my coffee. "One more year and we can drink together."

"Legally," I whisper and smile.

"Wait, hold on a second... something is different. I know that face," she says and then gasps in recognition. "That's a fresh orgasm face!"

"Skye, oh my god, shut the fuck up," I whisper.

"Did you and Sunshine...?" She asks, excited.

"No, Jesus," I blush.

"Okay so what did he do? Fingerbang? Eat you out?" She asks and I look away, smiling. "Oh my God, he did both."

"How the fuck do you do that?" I laugh.

"Tell me everything. How was it? Does he need work? I can teach him some tricks to do with his tongue," she giggles.

"Trust me, the man knows what he's doing with his tongue."

"Damn, Parker." She says to herself. "So what happened?!"

"It was a birthday present," I giggle. "But he wouldn't let me reciprocate *or* follow him to the shower."

"Okay I need to have a little talk with him about this whole striving for perfection thing because what *guy* won't *let* their girl reciprocate?!" She says, far too loudly.

"Skye, shut the hell up," I laugh.

"I say go for it. Get down on your knees like the dirty little slut you are and give that man the head of his life. And then go all the way so we can gush about it." She laughs.

My mouth drops open at her crassness and I playfully hit her in the arm. To be honest, it feels good to finally talk to someone about all of it.

My phone buzzes and I see a text from Sunshine.

Now shall commence the twenty reasons why I love you. You know… since you're twenty now. #1. You are literally one of the strongest, most resilient people I know. I can't wait to see you tonight.

"This man is perfection in a human," I say, smiling and Skye reads over my shoulder.

"Damn, Parker's got moves."

We both laugh and finish up our coffees before parting ways.

Each of the twenty reasons he texts me throughout the day melts my heart. If I didn't believe it before, I believe it now— this man *loves* me.

When I get home there are a dozen pink roses waiting on the island, a huge "Happy Birthday" balloon banner, and the kitchen table is set with rose petals and candles.

"Ah, the birthday girl. You're right on time." He smiles at me and then kisses me.

"Where are the guys?" I ask.

"I sent them away for the night. Come sit, I made dinner." Sunshine leads me to a chair and pulls it out for me.

I sit in the chair and smile at him. He puts plates of shrimp and noodles in front of us.

"I figured your favorite is a good choice for your birthday," he says, sitting across from me.

The dinner is perfect. After he cleans up, because of course I wasn't *allowed* to help, we sit on the couch close to each other and play *Left 4 Dead 2*.

"Oh, I almost forgot," Sunshine sits up as the round ends. He faces me and holds one of my hands. "Your final birthday present. Don't worry I'm not proposing."

He pulls a ring box out of his back pocket and hands it to me. I open it to reveal a beautiful rose gold band with a small topaz in the middle.

"I figured if you won't let me marry you because it's just a piece of paper or whatever, you can still have the jewelry that typically goes with it. There's no stress or anything," he says. "You can wear it on whatever finger you want on whichever hand you want. I just figured you still deserved a pretty ring."

"It's beautiful," I smile at him and put it on my left ring finger. "Thank you."

I kiss him deeply and move to sit in his lap, draping my legs over his.

"Now about that shower..." I say, and his control snaps.

In one swift movement, he wraps my legs around his waist and carries me to our bathroom, kissing me from my lips to my neck repeatedly. When he sets me down on the bathroom floor, we both impatiently tear at our clothes.

"I'm ready," I breathe. "I want you. All of you."

"Fuck," he says, elongating the word, before diving down to kiss me again.

He doesn't break the kiss to turn the shower on hot and pulls me in with him, still kissing me.

"Are you sure?" He asks.

"Positive," I moan.

He gently backs me into the shower wall and drops down to his knees, lifting one leg over his shoulder, as he buries his face between my thighs. He licks my clit slowly at first and then picks up momentum as I get closer and closer to the brink of orgasm. I grab a handful of his hair and moan loudly as I release onto his tongue. He stands slowly, keeping my leg in his grip, and kisses my neck as he slowly slides inside me. I grip his shoulder tightly as I get used to the feeling of him entering me as he slowly slides further in, kissing me and looking at me for any signs of discomfort. When he's fully inside me, there's a sense of absolute euphoria that takes over. I've never felt more safe or loved in my life. He takes his time with me, making sure I'm comfortable while simultaneously playing with my clit with his fingers. Only after I've came twice does he finally spill himself inside me, and for once, I actually like my birthday.

21

I'm draped across Sunshine's naked body as he plays with my hair, almost asleep when my phone rings.

"One of these days I'm going to turn my phone off when we have sex," I laugh and reach over to the nightstand where my phone is.

It's an unknown number so I let it go to voicemail, except they call right back. Who the hell needs me this badly at 11:00PM?

"Hello?" I answer, sleepily.

"Mia? Officer Bant here," he says and I shoot up in bed, Sunshine sitting up next to me.

"What is it?" He asks and I put the phone on speakerphone.

"Yes, Officer. How can I help you?" I ask.

"I'm so sorry to call so late, but I felt as though it was imperative you know," he says, "Are you familiar with a James Davis?"

"Yes... he's my ex... why?"

"Our suspect from the robbery over the summer, Axel Halcro, just named him as a man who hired him to do it."

"What?" I exclaim. "That's not possible. He's an asshole, sure, but he's not a psycho."

"We're trying to find him to bring him in for questioning," he says.

"Trying to find him... like you can't find him?"

"Someone must've given him a heads up. He hasn't been home for a few days."

I look at Sunshine in shock and horror.

"We're going to send a patrol car over to your home if you can give me your new address," Officer Bant says.

James did this? How? *Why?* I feel numb as Sunshine takes my phone and provides the address. Officer Bant relays some other information, but I can't focus on the words he's saying. Sunshine thanks him and hangs up.

"Mia?" He says, "Mia, baby, say something."

I can't. How could he do this to me? Did he ever really love me? Or is that why he did it? To get revenge? This is so out of character for him. Obviously I know he's a douchebag but I never thought he'd hire someone to scare me...

"Babe," Sunshine shakes me gently.

"How could he?" I ask.

"He's psychotic. We need to leave. I won't let him have the opportunity to get close to you."

I watch as Sunshine packs a bag for us and hear shouting outside. When I peek through the curtains of our bedroom to see what the commotion is, James is there. It doesn't take him long to notice me, making eye contact.

"There you are!" he yells. "Come down and talk to me for a minute!"

"Mia, stay here, I'll take care of this," Sunshine says and quickly heads down the stairs.

I follow after him and watch from a window in the living room, cracking it open slightly so I can hear them.

"Ahh Sunshine, why am I not surprised to see you?" James says.

"Get off my property," Sunshine replies.

"I mean, technically I'm on the sidewalk, which is *public* property," James sneers.

"Leave James. She doesn't want to see you."

I can hear in his tone that Sunshine is pissed, but trying to keep it under control.

"What is it you said, *Sunshine*? 'Come near her again and you'll be in the hospital'? Well, here I am, what are you waiting for?" James laughs and Sunshine shakes his head, which causes James to laugh harder.

"What a fucking pussy," He laughs and then yells, "Come on Mia, I'll show you what it's like to be with a real man!"

I feel tears falling down my face fast as I watch.

"Aww there you are sweetheart."

He notices me peeking through the window and takes a step forward, causing Sunshine to take a step toward him. I place my hand against the glass, watching the scene unfold and wanting so badly to reach out to Sunshine. To bring him inside.

"What's this?" James tilts his head as he studies me. "Did you fucking marry her?"

I pull my hand from the window quickly, realizing I had been touching the window with the hand that housed the ring Sunshine got me for my birthday.

"I did," Sunshine lies, smiling, "I give her what you never could."

James sneers and tackles Sunshine to the ground.

"No!!" I shout, grabbing my phone and quickly dialing the number that Officer Bant called me from.

"Mia? The off-"

"He's here!" I say. "He's at my house. They're fighting. Please tell them to hurry."

"On it. They should be there soon, Mia. Don't try to get involved. James is considered to be dangerous at this time."

"Justin! Asher!" I yell out.

At the panic in my voice, both guys rush down the stairs and check to see what I'm looking at through the window. We watch them wrestle on the ground for a minute. Sunshine has both height and strength on his side and flips James to the ground, sitting on top of him and punching him repeatedly in the face. I watch in horror, tears still falling quickly.

"Fuck," Justin says, jumping to his feet and heading out the door. "Parker, you got him dude. He's done. You're going to kill him."

Asher runs outside behind Justin. Between the two of them, they're able to pull Sunshine off of James, who is laying on the sidewalk moaning and bloody. When I run outside, police cars pull up. After they take in the scene, they call an ambulance and Sunshine cooperates as they put him in handcuffs.

"No!" I yell, running towards Sunshine. "James attacked him! It was self defense!"

"Mia, I'll be okay. It'll be okay. You're safe." Sunshine says. "Asher, can you get her inside, please?"

"No!" I yell as Asher puts an arm around me and leads me toward the house. "Ash get off of me!"

"Mia, come on, it's freezing out here," Asher says just before we get in the door.

"Just go inside babe, everything will be fine!" Sunshine yells as they move him toward the car, putting him in the back and driving off.

"What the fuck, Asher? I could have helped him!" I yell and push him away from me.

"Mia come on, the guy was unconscious and bloody. There was no way they were letting him go. He wanted you inside. He knows what he's doing."

"What do you mean he knows what he's doing?" I yell.

"This isn't the first time he's been arrested for fighting, Mia. You know him as this well put together, mature guy but he grew into that." Justin chimes in.

"How can I help him?" I ask.

"He'll call in a few hours to tell us how much bail is, and then we'll go bail him out."

I nod and stare out the window. The ambulance is loading James up on a stretcher. His whole face is bloody. I look away and cuddle up with a throw pillow on the couch. Romeo follows me to the couch and lays his head in my lap. I pet him for a few minutes until he falls asleep. Justin and Logan play *Dying Light* while we wait for Sunshine's call.

"He'll be alright, Mia, he always is." Logan says between rounds. I'm sure he can tell I'm mopey.

My phone rings.

"Hello?" I answer quickly, putting the phone on speaker.

"Mia." Sunshine breathes a sigh of relief on the other line.

"I'm so sorry." I cry.

"Sorry? Why are you sorry? Baby please don't cry. I'm not upset with you in the slightest. I don't have a lot of time to talk. Bail is set at one thousand dollars."

"A thousand? Damn man, that's way more than last time!" Justin exclaims and I hear Sunshine wince quietly.

"My debit card should be in my wallet on the nightstand. The PIN is 3850. Go to the ATM, take out a thousand, and bring it up to the Grinnell Police Station, please. I love you."

"I'll be there as soon as I can get there," I say, already heading upstairs.

"Be safe, don't drive too fast. And Mia?"

"Yeah?"

"I regret nothing. I will do anything to keep you safe."

"I love you," I say. "I love you so much."

"I have to go now. I'll see you s—."

The line disconnects.

I scramble to get Sunshine's ID and debit card together and head to the bank. I follow Sunshine's instructions and get a thousand dollars out as requested, then rush to the police station and head straight inside.

"I'm posting bail for Sunshine Parker," I rush.

"Okay, please take a seat over there." The lady behind the desk is unamused as she points to a row of chairs.

I sigh and walk over to a chair, sitting for what feels like an hour before she calls me back up to the desk. It's another twenty minutes before he finally walks out. I rush over to him and hug him around the neck and he grabs my waist with one arm, picking me up a little. He kisses my neck and buries his face in my hair.

"I'm so glad you're safe," he says.

I pull back to look at him and take in his injuries. He's got a black eye, a small cut along his left cheekbone, and a deeper cut above his right eyebrow. There's dried blood from the cut and his fist is swollen and bloody.

"I'm so sorry," I say, tears filling my eyes.

"Don't be sorry, but can we please get out of here?" he asks, kissing my temple and leading me toward the door.

He walks me around to the driver's side before getting himself in the passenger side, and I drive us to the nearest pharmacy.

"Do you need something?" He asks.

"You do. I'm going to grab some things to fix you up. Stay here."

"Mia it's three o'clock in the morning and we just found out that your ex *hired* someone to hurt you. You're not leaving my sight."

He unbuckles his seatbelt and follows behind me as I walk into the store.

I pick up some antibiotic cream as well as some gauze and butterfly bandages, paying quickly and holding Sunshine's unswollen hand the whole time. I hold his hand tight on the drive home, not wanting to go a single second without feeling his touch. When we walk in the house I head straight for our bathroom, pulling Sunshine with me. I push on his shoulder to have him sit on the toilet seat and grab a clean washcloth. He smiles up at me when I straddle his lap.

"This is the best nursing care I've ever received." He moves his hands to my hips and grinds me against him.

"Pervert," I laugh.

He squeezes my hip with his unbruised hand and plants a kiss on my collarbone while I gently clean his wounds with soap and water. The cut above his eyebrow is bleeding again so I hold some gauze over it. He's looking up at me and I can tell he's exhausted. I give him a small kiss and he lets out a breath.

"I'm so sorry this happened."

"Me, too. But you have nothing to be sorry about. That asshole is going to go straight from the hospital to jail. If he hadn't come here then he'd still be walking free."

When I place the butterfly bandage across the cut on his eyebrow, he winces.

"This is probably going to leave a scar. They should've taken you for stitches." I smirk, running my fingers over the bandage lightly.

"They say chicks dig scars. It just gives me some edge."

"I don't want you to have a permanent reminder of the pain he caused."

"It's not. It's a permanent reminder of my love for you. And how I'll do anything for you." He looks up at me and I kiss him again, this time longer.

His hands slide up my back as he kisses me back. He rubs his hands up and down my back a few times and then pulls me down to hug him.

"Come on, I need to hold you. I'm absolutely wiped."

We head for the bed and he pulls me into his arms.

"What if he presses charges?"

"He came at me first," he shrugs. "It was self-defense. I'm not worried about it. Now let's put this to rest for the night and get some sleep, okay?"

I nod and cuddle into him, ready for the night and this whole situation to be over.

22

After Skye and I found out that James had hired that guy to actually hurt both of us, but trashed the place when we weren't home, we somehow got closer. When she heard how Sunshine had kicked his ass, she *literally* cheered. The charges against Sunshine were dropped in self-defense and James is spending his time in jail with an upcoming trial, while we're all happier than ever. When I told my mom about James, she cried. She wants to fix our relationship, but I told her I wasn't sure I was ready. I'm trying to hold firm boundaries with her, though I do still see her every Saturday when I drop Frankie off.

Sunshine and I had just returned to the car when the dashboard lights up with Skye's name. We still talk frequently, though it has slowed a bit now that the semester started. She and Aubrey have both finally found jobs in their fields and they are *killing it* at adulting.

"Hello?" I answer in a singsong voice.

"Hey bitch, what are you doing?" She asks.

"I'm in the car with Sunshine. We just finished up book shopping."

"Perfect, so you're not busy, right?" She asks.

"Excuse you," Sunshine teases. "I resent that. We are very busy people."

"Oh shush Parker. Aubrey and I request both of your presence." She says with a slight accent to indicate formality.

"Oooookay? At your place?" I ask.

"Nope, I'm going to send you an address and I need you to be here in a half hour."

"That's cryptic," Sunshine laughs.

"Is everything okay?" I ask.

"Bye!" Skye replies and the line disconnects.

I look over at Sunshine briefly and he wears the same puzzled look I do. Once Skye texts the address, Sunshine adjusts the navigation system.

"Where does she have us going?" I ask, as Sunshine rests his hand on my thigh.

After a few minutes of looking down at his phone, he looks over at me, his head resting on the headrest.

"Some kind of government building?" He says, confused.

"I swear to god if they got themselves arrested, I'm not bailing them out." I laugh.

Sunshine holds my hand as we enter the building. I can honestly say I've never been inside of City Hall before, and now I'm kicking myself for it because it is *gorgeous*. The ceilings are incredibly high and let in a lot of natural light with all of the windows. Sunshine and I wander aimlessly, taking in all of the gorgeous architectural designs when we hear a low whistle. I turn to find Skye and Aubrey waving emphatically at us. In white dresses.

"Holy shit," I mumble.

"Hi!!!" Skye squeals as she hugs both of us.

"Are we here for what I think we're here for?" I ask and Aubrey nods, excitedly.

"What? What are we here for?" Sunshine asks, adorably confused.

"Sunshine Parker, welcome to our wedding," Skye gestures around city hall.

Sunshine looks at me with wide eyes and hugs Skye and Aubrey quickly.

The room within city hall where they perform wedding ceremonies is just another room, but the look on Skye's face when she vows to love Aubrey forever is enough to bring me to tears as Sunshine and I watch our best friends in the world get married. Sunshine wraps his arms around me from behind and kisses my cheek as Aubrey and Skye say "I do," brushing a tear away. When the official pronounces them wife and wife, Skye kisses Aubrey more passionately than I've ever seen and then turns to us, screeching in excitement.

"I'm married, bitches!" She yells, and then drags Aubrey over to us for a group hug.

Sunshine and I wait outside on a bench while Aubrey and Skye sign all of the legal paperwork that comes with getting married, his arm around my waist. The weather is getting colder, but Sunshine opens his zip up and wraps his arms around me so it's covering both of us.

"You know, today was amazing."

"Yeah? I can't believe they just up and decided to get married on a random Friday." Sunshine laughs.

"You know what?" I say. "I think I'm on board with marriage. With you. At some point."

"Yeah?" He turns me in his arms so he can see my face and I nod.

"I love you Sunshine. I want forever with you."

He places a soft hand on my cheek and kisses me.

"I love you, Mia. More than anything."

Epilogue

Sunshine is still sleeping next to me, shirtless and in only boxers, when I wake up. I kiss my way down his chest and kiss his hip.

"Mmm," he groans happily. "What are you doing?"

I smile against his hip and free him from his boxers. He gasps and another low groan emerges.

I take him in my mouth and work my hand around his base.

"Ah, Mia." He rasps, running a hand through my hair.

His build up is slow and I'm hungry for him. He finishes in my mouth and I lick it up, greedily. He pulls me up to him and crashes his lips on mine.

"Thank you," he says.

"Happy birthday," I giggle. "I hope you don't mind that I stole your gift idea."

"Not in the slightest. Are you okay?"

"I'm good," I nod. "Never better."

"I'm taking you to dinner tonight." He stretches and then curls himself around me.

"You mean I have to go on a *date* with you? On your *birthday?* When it's *freezing* outside? Fiiiiiiine," I tease.

"It'll be a good time," he whispers. "And then we can come back here and have an even better time, if you're up for it."

"Ah yes, do you want your present now or later?" I smile.

"You mean *that* wasn't my present?" he laughs.

"It was one of them, but I have an actual, tangible present too."

"Yessssss I love birthdays. Bring it to dinner?" He asks and I nod.

I text him random happy birthday messages throughout my last day of finals. I can't believe it's already the end of the semester.

When I arrive home, he has a suit on. I haven't seen him in a suit since he was in costume for *The Last Five Years* and I'm practically drooling as I stand in the doorway and stare at him.

"I love when you look at me like that." He smiles and walks over to kiss me. "We need to leave in 45 minutes for our reservation. I bought a new dress for you, it's on our bed."

I smile at him and kiss him back.

When I walk into our room there is a gorgeous red dress lying on the bed with a pair of black, fleece lined leggings and black heels. I love it when he thinks of everything. I grab a quick shower and change into the outfit.

"Babe!" I yell from the bedroom and Sunshine rushes up the stairs.

"What's wrong?" He asks.

"My ring. I put it right here on the nightstand and now it's gone." My vision blurs as tears fill my eyes.

"Baby it's okay, we'll find it. It has to be in here somewhere."

We scour the room with no luck and Sunshine frowns.

"We need to leave," he sighs.

"I'm so sorry." I frown. "I swear I laid it right here next to my bracelet."

"It's okay," he says. "I'm sure it'll turn up at some point."

"God, what kind of girlfriend am I? Losing my ring on your birthday?" I laugh sarcastically.

"Literally the best girlfriend. Don't worry so much," he kisses my temple and we leave for the restaurant.

I thought we'd be overdressed but I was wrong. The restaurant is *nice*. There are white tablecloths on every table and it's lit by candlelight. Fake candles of course, but still gorgeous. There are string lights hung through-out the restaurant. And the *food*. Probably the best food I ever had.

"So your birthday present," I say, and grab the bag at my feet.

"Thank you."

I watch as he opens the bag and pulls out the two playbills.

"I had that one made," I say. It's a playbill for Wicked with Sunshine's name listed for Fiyero alongside other famous Broadway actors, ads for Sunny Soaps, and a long, sappy dedication from me.

"This is so freaking cool." He smiles down at it.

"Yeah well I figured you'd want the first copy of you as Fiyero. They'll flood the market soon enough but-" I shrug.

He pulls out the other playbill and his eyes go wide. It's a 1985 opening night playbill for *Singin' in the Rain* signed by Don Correia, who played Don Lockwood.

"Wow." He exhales. "This is amazing. This must've cost you a fortune."

"Don't worry about that." I smile at him. The savings were worth it for the look on his face. "I figured it'll go well in your collection."

"It will, thank you so much."

When dessert comes, I'm so stuffed that I can hardly eat another bite.

"So listen, there's something I wanted to talk to you about," he says, but then drops his napkin on the floor.

"Smooth move," I tease.

He comes up on one knee in front of me when he bends to pick it up.

"Mia," he starts, smiling up at me.

Holy shit. What?!

"I love you more than anything in this world," he says and holds out my ring still grinning from ear to ear.

"The playbill is amazing, but there would be no better birthday present in the world than you saying you'll marry me. Will you please do me the honor?"

"Yes," I blurt out.

His smile deepens immediately as he slides my ring on my left ring finger and people at tables around us start clapping. I can hardly contain the blissful tears that fall, but Sunshine wipes them away and picks me up, giving me a quick twirl.

I don't know where the future is headed, but as long as I have Sunshine, it'll be amazing.

Acknowledgements

This book has been so many years in the making and I can't believe that I'm finally here, publishing my first novel!

First and foremost, I'd like to thank *you* for taking a chance on my debut novel. There are so many amazing books out there, and I am honored that you chose to read mine. I hope that you loved Mia and Sunshine as much as I have over the past few years.

To my alpha and beta readers—Erin, Becca, Angela— you were an integral part in making this dream a reality. Having you to bounce ideas off of, fix plot holes, deal with my many cry sessions of "what if it's not good enough," and point out when I'm being just a little bit crazy was essential. I would not have kept going without you.

To my husband, who has frequently tells me "if I'm going to bet on anyone getting shit done, it's you," who doesn't let me talk badly about myself, who does everything he can to convince me that I'm capable... Thank you for loving me and thank you for believing in me.

To my two beautiful girlies who are convinced that I can do *literally* anything. You are my reason for breathing.

To the rest of my family, who I won't name specifically because I'm going to inevitably leave someone out and I don't want to— I love you all. Thank you for believing in me, encouraging me, and putting up with my emotional ass.

Finally to Shannon, who has helped me navigate the (terrifying) world of social media and marketing.

I know for a fact that I'm probably missing people, but if you know me like I think you do, you know it's not intentional and that I still love you just as much!

About the Author

Leigh Sharp is a contemporary romance author living near Chicago, IL. She is a fierce advocate for both mental health and those with intellectual and developmental disabilities. When she's not writing, you'll typically find her hanging out with her two kiddos, working in the mental health field, or reading. She is a graduate of Western Illinois University where she studied music therapy, but she has been an avid writer since high school.

To learn more about Leigh's work, visit her website at leighsharpauthor.com or slide into her DMs on TikTok, Instagram, or Facebook.

www.ingramcontent.com/pod-product-compliance
Lightning Source LLC
Chambersburg PA
CBHW020134120726
47903CB00007B/2251